The shrieking wind and blowing snow made it difficult for Briggs to see anything from the bank of the roadway where he stood. Quickly, he crossed to the other side and plunged into the birch forest. Edging forward cautiously, he managed to discern the lighted windows inside Gamov's compound.

As Briggs watched from the darkness of the woods, a back door opened and two uniformed men —rifles slung over their shoulders—marched out into the open. Evidently, Gamov took his security seriously. This is what Briggs had hoped to learn.

If Gamov was this security conscious, then he'd start to get paranoid when he realized he was being followed by an enemy cohort. Paranoid types often make mistakes. Incriminating mistakes. It would all add up in Brezhnev's mind when it came time for Gamov's trial for treason.

Smiling to himself, Briggs turned back—straight into two more guards, their assault rifles trained on him.

"Good evening," he said pleasantly, making no move to raise his hands. His stiletto was hidden in the folds of his coat.

"Put your hands on your head!" one of the guards snapped. The other pulled out a walkie-talkie and raised it to his lips.

"Wait!" Briggs cried out in alarm.

The guard with the radio hesitated, and in that moment, they were all closer to death than any of them knew . . . .

DAVID
BANNERMAN THE
MAGIC
MAN
THE
GAMOV
FACTOR
#2

ZEBRA BOOKS
KENSINGTON PUBLISHING CORP.

ZEBRA BOOKS

are published by

KENSINGTON PUBLISHING CORP.
475 Park Avenue South
New York, N.Y. 10016

Printed in the United States of America

For Laurie

PROLOGUE

The bulky, black limousine purred up the long, curving drive toward the imposing building that sprawled between two small birch forests outside Moscow. Built for aristocracy before the Revolution as a refuge from the heat and smells of the capital city in summer, ravaged by war and then neglect, it had been restored to its former splendor and presented to Ilya Alexandrovich Gamov as a reward for his loyalty and service, and as a mark of his high rank. To call it simply a dacha was gross understatement, and in fact, few did. It was Ilya's Palace to even the common man; everyone knew Gamov was the number three man at the Kremlin, with aspirations for first place, trusted by the ailing Leonid Brezhnev.

The limousine pulled up near a side entrance, under what had formerly been a protective arch between the main house and a small, subsidiary

7

carriage house. The driver jumped gingerly from the car. He carried no passenger, but brought from the rear seat a small package wrapped in brown paper and sealed with red wax, an ornate G design pressed into it.

The driver had no need to knock; the door was opened to him before he had made the steps, and he was greeted by a dark-haired young man, no more than twenty-six or twenty-seven, who had obviously been waiting for him.

"This is the delivery from Makarov, then?" the young man inquired, holding out his hand to accept the package. There was a tired resignation in his voice, rather than the elation the driver had expected.

"It is," the driver said. He placed the package in the young man's hand. "He said to tell you it's the best quality yet for sound and clarity." He waited for some reaction, perhaps a question, or at the very least the courtesy of a thank you, then turned to leave as none was forthcoming.

As he opened the limousine door he called back to the young man, who was re-entering the dacha, "Makarov will want to know what he thinks when he's finished with it."

The young man nodded and went inside. The driver shrugged, climbed back into the limousine and left.

Inside, the young man walked quietly along one of the two central halls on the first floor that crosscut the building, coming at length to the massive, central foyer. Shaped like an inverted bowl, ornately decorated with murals, gold

8

etchings and hand-carved woodwork, it seemed more museum than residence. The presence of a small desk next to the wide, marble stairs that swept down from the second floor in an arc was jarring and out of place, but necessary. Three shifts of security people were required to protect the master of this house each day, whether he was in residence or working in Moscow. The captain of each shift directed his men from this vantage point, making full use of radio communications and a bank of small television screens with which to monitor the corridors and grounds.

The captain of this evening's shift, Uri Provnenko, a bluntly-built man of forty-five, looked up as the young man approached. The motion flipped his unruly brown hair up at the crown, and when he moved again, his hair stayed the same in spite of the lanolin cream he had layered into it.

"We have another bit of entertainment, Reza?" he asked. The young man nodded. Not very talkative tonight, Provnenko thought. He did not care whether Reza was an aide to Gamov or not; he didn't like Muslims, didn't trust them, and didn't think they belonged in sensitive positions.

"Will you be taking it up to him?" Provnenko prodded.

"I suppose so," Reza said flatly. "We will need the video equipment."

"It's still there from the last time. In the study antechamber." Those dark, dark eyes, he thought, impossible to read. No way to tell what's going on behind them. No way to know what he

9

thinks or what he might be planning.

Reza walked slowly, resignedly up the staircase, looking straight ahead all the way, then turned to the right when he reached the top. The second floor corridor, running across the house, was more subdued in decoration than the first floor, but plush and formal nonetheless. Oak chair rails bisected the walls between floor and ceiling, with gold-swirled paper on the top and polished oak on the bottom. Heavy wooden doors broke the pattern of the hall in both directions, and at intervals there were chairs for security personnel on watch.

These extreme precautions were not usually required. It was normally sufficient to maintain the monitors and roving patrols of both house and grounds, but, on some occasions, Gamov felt the need of armed men just outside his door: for special interviews with special Politburo members and other high-ranking citizens.

Reza stopped at the second-to-last door on the left, hesitated, then rapped sharply three times.

"Enter," Gamov said from within. He was not a man to waste words.

"Makarov's video cassette is here," Reza told Gamov, or rather, his back, as he entered the man's private study. Gamov was seated behind a large, walnut desk, his leather-upholstered chair swiveled around toward the wall.

"Excellent," Gamov said, swinging around to face Reza. He placed his elbows on the desk and leaned forward, his gray eyes coming to life. Reza had noticed that about his superior early on, that those gray eyes seemed dead until the scent of prey—skewered and helpless—sparked life into them. It was a sick and twisted life; Reza preferred the flat, slate-colored stare of the ranking bureaucrat.

"I'll just go into the antechamber, then," Reza told him, crossing the room. The study had at some time in the distant, Czarist past been the quarters of a doubtless-devoted nanny, and the antechamber, a nursery for her small charge. The only entry and exit to that room was through the study—Gamov's main reason for choosing this as his primary work room at the dacha.

Gamov followed his aide, stretching as he stood to his full height, just a shade over six-four. Slender and muscular, with thick but perfectly-groomed silver hair, Gamov could incite fear in the broadest, most hardened men. It was not so much his physical presence, for at fifty-four some stooping of the shoulders could be detected. No, he seemed instead to give off a not-quite-definable aura of impending devastation. He was a lean and hungry . . . and dangerous man.

Reza switched on a table lamp adjacent to two comfortable chairs, arranged before a small television set. Nearby, with leads attached to the monitor, was a video recorder/player, one of the newer advances in Soviet technology, not yet available to the masses. Gamov seated himself as Reza slipped the cassette into place and started the tape. The image of a small bedroom came onto the screen, and Gamov reached for the lamp, turning it off.

"I want to miss nothing, not one detail," he said, as if the lack of light would enhance the screen image. Reza silently seated himself next to Gamov.

"Look." Gamov tapped Reza's knee, but kept his eyes on the screen.

Reza saw a plain room, probably in a hotel or nondescript apartment somewhere in Moscow, with a double bed in central position, a nightstand nearby, and a door on the far side of the bed. The door opened, slowly, and a man and woman came into view. Both were nude. The man was behind the woman, with one hand on her breast.

"Chernyev," Reza whispered, shocked, though he should not have been. He had seen enough films, videos and stills in this room to make the most naive person turn sarcastic. But he had never expected to see Ivan Chernyev in any of them. He had been Brezhnev's first appointment to the Politburo. A shining example of the best the Revolution could produce, beyond reproach, immune to blackmail by virtue of his dedication and morality.

"There is more," Gamov said pointing to the television, redirecting Reza's attention.

As Chernyev sprawled across the bed, the woman took the aggressive role, licking and biting her way down his chest to his groin. The movement off to the side of the screen caught Reza's eye, and he watched as another woman, blond and slender and good looking like the first, joined the pair on the bed, straddling Chernyev's face, then running her hands through the politician's hair to direct his movement.

"This is hardly in keeping with Chernyev's solid, grandfatherly image," snickered Gamov. The figures shifted positions, and Gamov remarked in delight, "See the belly? He's soft . . . soft and fat and off guard." He tapped Reza rapidly on the arm. "The sound. Turn it louder."

Reza obeyed, and the moaning of the people on screen filled the room. Chernyev reached orgasm, the proof of which showed around the mouth of the first woman they had seen. The other woman—they were so alike, they could be twins—would not let Chernyev go just yet, not until she, too, had been satisfied.

"Virna," they heard the first woman whisper, pulling at her accomplice and flopping next to Chernyev on her back. "Do not forget me." She parted her legs and held out her arms. The second woman, pulled herself off and kissed her deeply, while Chernyev directed himself to her satisfaction.

"Does this excite you . . . just a little?" Gamov asked Reza, looking at him peripherally, but missing nothing on the screen.

"Not particularly." Reza did not turn toward his superior to answer, yet he replied honestly. He had seen too much of this kind of thing to be titillated by it.

"Women," Gamov said with disgust. "Breeding stock, that is their purpose. They cannot offer the things a man needs. They cannot understand a man." He stood abruptly, turned off the video and rewound the tape, then handed it to

Reza. "Add this to our collection," he instructed.

Reza strode back into the study and stepped behind Gamov's desk. Only he and Gamov knew the combination to the safe secreted behind the wall there, a safe so large that it could constitute a small room in its own right. It had been built at Gamov's direction, to his specifications, and would only open when the correct codes had been punched into a numbered electronic device mounted under the desk.

Reza pushed the series and stood back as the wall slid to one side, then he stepped into the vault.

It was fireproof, bombproof and watertight, perfect for preserving Gamov's most valued documents, tapes, films and photographs for centuries —though far less time would elapse before the contents would be put to use.

Everything was labeled with subject, date and a summary of contents, stacked in alphabetical order on steel shelves.

Reza pulled a pen from his vest pocket and marked the date and Chernyev's name on the cassette. He paused and added: *ménage a trois*. It sounded less vulgar in French, somehow, than it would have in Russian. He felt ill. Chernyev had been his hero from the time he was a youngster, though he had never had an opportunity to know the man personally. This was a man above corruption, an ideal to be emulated. Reza sighed. Another fallible, aging, overweight fool trying to live out his fantasies while he was able. And playing right into Gamov's hands. He wondered how long it would take Gamov to arrange a private conference here with Chernyev, and whether he would feel the need of guards at the door when they met.

"I have them all, now." Gamov's voice behind him made Reza jump; he hadn't heard him approach, had been too involved in his own thoughts.

"All?" he echoed. He placed the cassettes on the appropriate shelf, then turned toward Gamov.

"The Politburo," Gamov replied. "Five seats vacant, and I have all the opposition now, with Chernyev. It will be mine."

"But the military . . ." Reza reminded him.

"Enough. I have enough of them, one way or the other." He nodded toward the shelves lining the vault. He looked intently at Reza, straight through him, it seemed. "And you are disturbed about this?"

"Disappointed." Reza chose his words carefully. "I admired Chernyev. So did my father. I thought he was above such behavior."

"There may have been a certain amount of, shall we say, cooperation, from the women we saw tonight," Gamov admitted. "How else could we have convinced Chernyev to assist us with recording our entertainment? But no one forced him into anything, and one must wonder how many such instances have occurred over the years, perhaps on a regular basis." He let Reza digest this, then put an arm around the young man's shoulder, nudging him out of the vault.

"The root of Chernyev's problem is obvious,"

Gamov continued as they stepped back into the study. "Women." He pushed a series of numbered buttons under the desk and the wall slid back into place. "That is one area where your traditions are well founded. Keep them apart, cover them up, don't be distracted by them." He smiled suddenly, sending a chill down Reza's spine.

"It's getting late, sir . . ." Reza began, but was cut off.

"You are correct. We shall retire, then." He strode to the door, opened it, then turned back to his aide. "Turn off the light. I will wait for you."

ONE

Sir Roger Hume, M.P., dozed comfortably in his wing chair before a flickering fire, the first of the season on this crisp, September evening. He was finally, fully enjoying his semi-retirement at his estate, the one place in the world where he could feel completely at ease. It had been a pleasant, uneventful day. He'd ridden his favorite horse, Briarcliff of Finchley—who had cost him a fortune and proved too weak at the shin to race, but whose courage he vastly admired—then sat for some time with his daughter, Sylvia, going over correspondence from his constituents. He'd noticed the slight chill in the air at about the time cook brought in the tea tray and Sylvia decided she had to dash off on some errand or other before dinner. It rather delighted him. A crackling fire warmed the soul as well as the body, and he realized how much he had missed that during the summer months. He had sipped his tea, sampled some cinnamon biscuits, enjoyed a pipe despite his doctor's dire warnings of its effect on his health, then gradually nodded off as he watched the flames lick at the three logs he had stacked in the hearth.

Cook had come for the tray, found him sleeping and warned Sylvia not to disturb him when she returned.

"I wouldn't dream of it," Sylvia reassured her. "Poor love, he's been so busy all his life, it's time he was able to live at a leisurely pace." She sighed, pushing her long, dark hair back from her face, and added, "It seems so far from London, here. I only wish it were farther still."

"True, true," clucked cook in agreement. A rotund, plain woman, she had served the family from the time Sir Roger and Lady Caroline had married, through Sylvia's childhood and the tragedy of Lady Caroline's lost battle with cancer, watching him run the family business and the business of government at the same time, over-extending himself, worrying that he would leave Sylvia an orphan. It was with relief that cook saw him slow his pace now, spend more time with his daughter, though she was fully an adult at twenty-five and quite capable of living independently.

It was Sylvia, passing through the entry foyer of the large house, who happened to hear an automobile approaching. At the door she peered into the gathering dusk but was unable to identify the vehicle. That worried her. Strange autos too often brought demands upon Sir Roger, and she was

18

anxious to protect him from any strains. He deserved his rest. He might be only in his mid-sixties—and at that, sensitive about his age and any implication that it might impair his abilities—but he was her father, she loved him and wanted to look out for him. She stepped out the door when she saw a figure emerge from the auto, ready to run interference.

Sylvia peered intently as a short, stocky figure moved briskly toward her, then shrieked with surprise and recognition.

"Uncle Rudy!" She dashed down the steps to give the man a hug and kiss, which were warmly reciprocated. "You should have rung up first and said you were coming. Is Aunt Marta with you?"

"No, not this trip, Sylvia. But next time, I promise." He wrapped an arm around her shoulders and the two walked up to the house. Something in his voice, as well as a tension in his body, told her that this was not a social call.

"You're here on business, then." It was a statement rather than a question, and he nodded. Rudyard Howard and Sir Roger Hume were bound as closely by matters of state—intelligence matters affecting both Great Britain and the United States—as they were by years of friendship.

"I caught a seat on the Concord, leased a motorcar and dashed out here," he told her as he held the door for her. "I must be back on the next return flight of the bird." He was taken aback, as he always was when he first saw her after an absence, by her resemblance to her mother, Lady

Caroline. Sylvia was a beauty, though rather spoiled, particularly since her mother's demise.

"We'll just go and wake him," Sylvia said, leading the way toward Sir Roger's study. "He's having a bit of an after-tea and before-dinner nap." She paused before opening the door. "Don't put him through such paces this time, please, Uncle Rudy." Then she turned and left, leaving Rudyard Howard to business with her father.

Sir Roger was still dozing lightly, his silver-topped head bobbing gently toward his chest, as Howard walked quietly to the wing chair and cleared his throat. It had the desired effect, bringing Sir Roger around quickly.

"Rudy, old chap!" he exclaimed in surprise, coming up from the chair and extending his right hand in greeting at the same time. "What brings you round unannounced?"

"Business," Howard replied, "though it's always a pleasure to see you, and of course, Sylvia. She met me at the door." His expression was grim, though he was sincere in his affirmation of the bond between them.

"Do sit, then, and we'll discuss it." Sir Roger pulled the upholstered chair from behind his desk over to the fire and gestured for Howard to be seated.

"The Agency has come up with several bits of information that, taken together, could spell serious problems for the West—all the western countries," Howard began as soon as he sat down. "You've heard the name Gamov before?

Ilya Alexandrovich Gamov?"

"A fairly powerful man in the Soviet Union," Sir Roger replied. He reached for his pipe and emptied it, preparatory to a smoke. This could be a three-pipe briefing. "He's estimated to be holding the number three or number four position, depending upon which analyst is assigning his importance, behind Brezhnev."

"Yes, and our information shows that he may be pushing himself up faster than that, to, say, the number two position, directly behind Brezhnev." Sir Roger's eyebrows shot upward at this, something Howard did not miss. "He's an ambitious man, hard line, and has no reservations as to which methods he'll use to secure power for himself."

"That's hardly a distinction in the Kremlin," Sir Roger pointed out.

"He goes beyond the usual power plays," Howard asserted, "and he is firmly in the favor of Brezhnev. Look." He opened the small, diplomatic pouch he had kept tucked under one arm ever since leaving Dulles Airport, and pulled out a sheaf of papers. "These are reports from various operatives regarding different members of the military and the Politburo. Each alone would mean little, but taken together, as I said before, they could tell an ominous story. This one, for example." He set a brief report on top of the slim stack, and read aloud from it.

" 'General Gordonyev did little over the past year to hide his disdain for Gamov. Following his receipt from Hastings on 3 August 1982 of four pairs Levi jeans, Gordonyev has changed attitude entirely. Refuses any contact with Hastings. Was known to have had conference with Gamov at Gamov's dacha on 5 August 1982. Suspect Gamov learned of gift and is using this against him.' And here's another.

'' 'Chernyev'—that's Ivan Chernyev, Politburo —'approached repeatedly by Virna Fedyenko between 6 June 1982 and 31 August 1982, following introduction by Makarov at Bolshoi performance, 22 May 1982. Known to have had meeting with Gamov at Gamov's dacha on 3 September 1982. Makarov known operative of Gamov. Chernyev former supporter of Andropov, gave pro-Gamov speech at Politburo meeting on 5 September 1982. Suspect connection.' ''

"In short," said Sir Roger, "it would appear that Gamov is blackmailing his opponents into supporting him, instead of Andropov, as successor to Brezhnev." He relit his pipe, drew on it and let a small puff of smoke rise above his head. "It's an old but effective means to concentrate one's power and further one's ambitions. If your people have made these connections, surely Brezhnev and Andropov have as well."

"We don't believe Brezhnev has." Howard shook his head vigorously. It was serious business, and he took it with deadly seriousness. "He's ill, not so sharp as he once was in matters like this. Gamov was his protégé. He's not inclined to believe the worse of him, even if someone were to approach him with evidence of it."

"And Andropov?" Sir Roger inquired. Howard

could only shrug his shoulders.

"He's in a most delicate position. At this moment, perhaps he would succeed Brezhnev. It has come already to a point where his succession is not a certainty. We simply do not have sufficiently close contacts with Andropov's staff to make a determination. And we are concerned that Andropov is either not fully aware of the situation, or in a position where he cannot take drastic action without destroying himself in the process."

"I see," Sir Roger mused. "Andropov may know that Gamov is attempting to undermine his support by threatening to bump skeletons from important closets, but if he has Gamov eliminated, he will never take over when Brezhnev dies. He'd be pinned with it first thing, disgraced, banished or executed."

"And it is of the greatest importance to the West, and to the cause of peace, that Andropov, not Gamov, succeed Brezhnev." Howard spoke slowly, giving emphasis to each word.

"Then there is more than the blackmailing going on," Sir Roger stated. He knocked the ashes from his pipe.

"Definitely. Problem is," Howard admitted, "we aren't sure just what the specifics are. We do know that Gamov has long been an advocate of nuclear buildup. He has done everything in his considerable power to block SALT II, and has pushed for stockpiling while the diplomats dicker, so that they are that much further ahead when and if a freeze is implemented.

"Moreover, we have numerous reports that he's

could only shrug his shoulders.

directing some top secret project at the Gorky Missile Base. Higher than top secret, actually, compartmentalized intelligence level. That's why we can only get bits and pieces, and have not been able to make them fit yet. He alone knows it all; the personnel at the missile base each knows only so much as is necessary to carry out his individual function. Gathering firm data on him is most difficult.''

"I don't like it." Sir Roger's brow knit in concentration and disturbance. "Have your people or the Agency been able to draw a psychological profile?"

"The Agency did. I brought a copy along." Howard shuffled through the papers in his lap and fished out the one he sought.

"The first two pages are computerized data. The third page is the interpretive report," he explained, handing it to Sir Roger.

Sir Roger began scanning the material. "The experts are inclined to think poor Ilya suffers from psychoses, paranoia ranking first, followed closely by delusions of grandeur." He looked up from the report. "A man such as he could annihilate the human race."

"Precisely."

"And are you here for my advice? Do you want to know how I think you should handle this problem?" Sir Roger inquired.

"In part," Howard hedged diplomatically. He was, after all, with the State Department, and had learned to measure his words to avoid slighting anyone. "We have something of a plan in mind,

24

but I would first like to hear your views."

Sir Roger's pipe had gone out, the only disadvantage of pipes when compared with cigars or cigarettes. He relit it and puffed contemplatively before responding.

"I should think it would create more problems than it would solve to terminate Gamov. It's not that it would be that difficult to remove him, though it would likely require an assassin with a death wish. But the balance of power within the Kremlin would be thrown to the winds. Andropov could be blamed, particularly if it's true that Gamov is conducting large-scale blackmail operations against the most powerful men in the Soviet Union and evidence were uncovered after his demise. Yes, it would look black indeed for Andropov. Not that any successor will be in our pockets," he added, "but we know where we stand with Andropov. Anyone else is an unknown factor at best.

"Nor can we expose any blackmailing that he's been up to," Sir Roger continued. "He's a favorite of Brezhnev, giving him the advantage, and it would only serve to destroy the victims of the blackmailing. After all, each of them has acted in some way counter to the Revolution; that's what Gamov would have on them. We could end out making him look better and ensuring his succession to power. And unless we can obtain clearer information regarding his activities at Gorky Missile Base, there's no gain in bringing that to Brezhnev's attention. It would merely appear that the man is actively protecting the interests of the proletariat."

Sir Roger shifted in his chair, set the pipe in an ashtray next to him and leaned earnestly toward his friend and ally.

"But we could set him up for a downfall. If we can't lure him into a position of weakness, as he has done with those he has blackmailed, then we can frame him. Make him look the traitor. It would have to be very good indeed to hold up, but there appears no other effective way. That, or sit back helplessly and hope all works out well without our efforts."

For the first time since his arrival in England, a smile broke across Howard's face.

"You have just summarized our approach," he said simply.

"That's all well and good," Sir Roger replied. He reached again for the pipe. "But I see no reason to seek my counsel or involve me in this. Obviously, you have a plan in mind, and I will tell you at the outset that I'm not inclined to sneak into Russia to personally carry it out for you. Why this visit?"

"You're right. We have a plan. In a nutshell, we want to set up Gamov to appear to be a traitor of the worst sort. It's a nearly impossible task . . ." Howard's voice trailed off.

"And you need someone who can do the impossible. You need a 'magic man,' " Sir Roger finished Howard's sentence.

"Right again. Our operative must be fluent in Russian and probably a number of other East European and Baltic languages. No accent, none.

He must know the tradecraft. He must be something of a con artist, a quick thinker, a born actor, a man who can pass for a member of any class level at any time."

"My dear man," Sir Roger pointed out, "you have just such a man on your payroll now. Briggs—Donald O'Meara is the chap you need for this job. Remember the Popov affair? Rudy, who else could have managed that? You rewarded him with U.S. citizenship and steady employment. He's already yours."

"O'Meara's just on the edge of intelligence now," Howard pointed out. "Because we both promised him that we would not call upon him for this type of work again. Do you know what he does for us now? He recruits guides and interpreters for visiting foreign dignitaries. I rather believe he enjoys his work, too," Howard added with a chuckle. "These interpreters are by and large female, chosen for their looks as much as for their fluency in foreign languages. They're quite useful in terms of gathering information for us. But they don't report intelligence to O'Meara. He simply signs them on and, in conjunction with our intelligence division and the Agency, sends them off on individual assignments. He's been very firm about that. No more risks."

"I'm afraid I can't help you, then," Sir Roger said, lighting his pipe again. "I know of no one else who could handle such an assignment."

"O'Meara trusts you. You have a rapport with him," Howard went on, as if Sir Roger hadn't spoken. "Perhaps, if you spoke with him, explained the urgency of the situation, he would consider doing it.''

''If he's as adamant as you say, I doubt that I could persuade him,'' Sir Roger pointed out. ''But the least I could do is try.''

''I knew I could count on you.'' Howard beamed broadly. ''We leave on the statesbound Concord flight tomorrow.''

''Not without me!'' Sylvia's voice brought both men around suddenly to where she stood in the doorway.

''How long have you been there?'' demanded Sir Roger. It truly incensed him that his daughter would eavesdrop on his conversations. It worried him, too, that she would learn more than she should know, place herself in harm's way as the price of that knowledge.

''Long enough,'' she replied, walking leisurely to the hearth and placing herself between the men and the fire. ''Long enough to know that Briggs is involved again. And that if you're going to see him, I am going to see him.''

''And how much more have you learned?'' asked Howard. He shared Sir Roger's concerns about Sylvia.

''That you want to send Briggs back into Russia, nothing more. And that if he goes, it's dangerous, and he may not return. So,'' she concluded with a toss of her head, ''I want to see him before that happens.''

''I did not have the impression that you and Briggs were on such amicable terms,'' her father pointed out.

"Sometimes we are, and sometimes we're not," she admitted with a shrug. "I suppose that's why I want to see him. Don't worry Father, I shan't try to dissuade him. No one can dissuade him from a course, once he's decided on it."

"What do you think, then, Rudy?" inquired Sir Roger.

"I think that Marta would be thrilled to have both of you as our guests," Howard answered. "In fact, I have three seats reserved for tomorrow's flight back." He looked at Sylvia. "Marta told me I'd never get Sir Roger out of here without you, and she is right again, as ever."

"Mr. O'Meara, you have a call on line three," Dora Winchester's voice announced through the intercom on Briggs' desk. "Mrs. Rudyard Howard."

The mention of Howard's name brought Briggs fully to attention, away from the state dinner guest list he'd been studying in the hope of making the right match between guest and interpreter. Though Howard was technically his boss, he had had little contact with the man since wrapping up the Popov matter, and didn't particularly care to.

"Who did you say is calling?" he asked, pressing the button marked CM that allowed communication between himself and his secretary.

"Mrs. Rudyard Howard," Dora repeated. "Do you want me to get her number and tell her you'll call back?"

"No, I'll take the call. Thank you, Dora." *Mrs.*

Howard. He remembered her from their first introduction, a quiet, hospitable woman who kept to the background. What could she possibly want with him? He punched into line three and put the receiver to his ear.

"Mrs. Howard? Donald O'Meara here. What can I do for you?"

"On the contrary, Mr. O'Meara, we would like to do for you," Marta told him. "We are having a small dinner party here tomorrow evening, and would be honored if you would join us. It's quite informal. Thought we should enjoy the last of the good weather before winter sets in, and have some friends here to share it."

Briggs hesitated. He was not one of Howard's friends. There must be a catch in it somewhere, and Howard was damnably clever having his wife extend the invitation. It hamstrung Briggs. He could hardly demand that Marta tell him the real reason he was wanted in their home, nor could he rudely refuse the invitation. Besides, it piqued his curiosity.

"I would enjoy that immensely," he told her. "What time shall I arrive, and is there anything that I can bring?"

"Just bring yourself and a hearty appetite, about seven," Marta said. "As I mentioned, it's informal. Weather permitting, we would like to dine outdoors. You do recall how to get here?"

"Of course," he assured. "Georgetown Pike. It's quite convenient for me. I'll see you then."

He replaced the receiver in its cradle and tried to return to the business at hand, but could no longer concentrate. Something was afoot. He tried calling Rudyard Howard at his office, but got only as far as Howard's secretary. Mr. Howard was out of the office on business and not expected back before the close of the day. He did not leave a message.

Dora interrupted his musings with the afternoon mail, setting it lightly on his desk and leaving. She could recognize his pensive moods, and knew not to bother him at such times. Briggs sifted through the stack of letters, then dropped them back onto the desk. Swiveling around in his chair, he set one hand on the small safe in the corner, tapping a rhythm with his fingers, then finally deciding to open it. He had relinquished all the paraphernalia of the trade—the phony passports, forged documents—in exchange for citizenship, a safe job, roots. All the paraphernalia save one thing. The stiletto was still there, just where he had set it when he took this office, its handle wrapped in the same twine he'd bought for it back to Soho, just after his first kill. The twine gave him a better grip, a deadlier grip.

Briggs reached for it now, felt the weight, checked the balance in his hand. Still holding the stiletto, he swiveled back to the desk. There was no choice but to wait until tomorrow evening to find out what Howard really wanted with him. He shrugged and began methodically slicing open his mail with the blade.

TWO

As the Concord slowed to subsonic speed and came inland toward Dulles, Sylvia was surprised at how few of the trees she could make out below her had taken on bright, fall foliage. The States had such odd weather. In late September, one would expect to see a crazy quilt of color, but not, Howard had reminded her since she'd been a child, in the South. She watched intently as they passed over rows of track homes, neatly laid out along meandering streets, able to spot the Potomac River in the distance. Her father and Rudyard Howard were seated several rows away. Since she could not apply herself to eavesdropping on their conversation, she would occupy approach time with the scenery below.

The runway surprised her. It seemed they were floating quietly along, well in the air, when suddenly there was a small wood off to one side and the concrete of the runway before them. She'd never flown the Concord before. Everything about it was too fast for comprehension.

The plane was met by one of Dulles' distinctive ground transports, a quasi-bus that could move up and down to the level of planes in order to embark and disembark passengers. Sylvia made certain she was with both Howard and Roger as they left the plane, and she sat between them on the way to the terminal.

"We'll have to keep her occupied and out of harm's way," Sir Roger whispered to his friend as Howard led them through customs. "I'm afraid Sylvia is too curious for her own good."

"Marta will see to that," Howard assured him.

They were met by a dark blue Ford bearing government plates, and Sir Roger immediately recognized the driver from his previous involvement in the Popov affair.

"Mr. Chiles, how very good to see you again. I don't believe you ever had a proper introduction to my daughter," he said as he followed Sylvia into the rear of the car and Howard climbed into the front seat. "Sylvia, this is Bob Chiles. Bob, this is Lady Sylvia Hume."

"Pleased to meet you," Chiles said over his shoulder. Sylvia could see little of him save a healthy head of brown hair atop a set of wide shoulders and an apparently well-kept frame. She did not respond. She was unaccustomed to being formally introduced to chauffeurs. The States had odd weather and odd practices; Sylvia didn't care for either.

Chiles exited the Dulles Access Road at the first opportunity, turning left onto Route 28. The Access Road made him nervous—too few off ramps, and if one had to turn around, no way off before the airport. He shortcut through Sterling Park, along its rolling boulevard lined with repetitive versions of the same seven or eight styles of homes, to Leesburg Pike, then right to Dranesville and onto Route 193, Old Georgetown Pike. Sir Roger and Sylvia both found this road the most familiar, more English than many an English country lane, twisting through woods and over creeks, with an occasional view available to the sharp eye of secluded estates.

Rudyard Howard owned such an estate, just off 193 and along the Potomac. It was set far enough back from the road that even the keenest eye could not see it. Howard not only valued his privacy on a personal level, he also required it on a professional level.

Marta Howard was waiting for them on the front steps when they arrived, a lightweight shawl around her shoulders to protect her from the slight chill in the air. Howard kissed her, Sir Roger pecked her cheek, and Sylvia wrapped her arms around her in a warm embrace.

"Sylvia, you must come with me and freshen up, and get me caught up on everything that's been going on in your life," Marta told her. "We haven't had a good visit in such a long time." Marta turned briefly to her husband. "Dinner is at seven, dear, and we do have a guest this evening." She then directed Sylvia inside, focusing the young woman's attention elsewhere.

Briggs pulled out of the underground parking garage beneath his apartment building, revving the engine of his Porsche for good measure, and eased into traffic. He lived in Georgetown; it would take him only a few minutes to arrive at Howard's estate. It had been difficult making himself wait until 6:45. He was insatiably curious, and Marta Howard's invitation had fueled the fires. At the same time, he didn't want to appear overly anxious. Calm, he told himself, catching the reflection of his blue eyes in the rear view mirror. Calm, cool, collected.

A maid greeted him at Howard's door, and led him through the house to the rear patio/porch, where she said the others were enjoying cocktails. Briggs spotted them before he stepped onto the patio, and everything began to click. Howard. Sir Roger. Sylvia. Yes, Sylvia, for good measure, and she had grown more beautiful, if that was possible. He paused for just a moment while the maid held the door for him, sensing a trap, wanting to run, feeling betrayed just seeing them all together again. They had *promised* him, never would he have to repeat the heroics required of him in the Popov matter.

"Mr. O'Meara," Marta Howard's soft voice behind him startled him. "Would you care for a cocktail?" She had apparently been returning from the kitchen, checking the last details of dinner. She was a most disarming woman.

35

"Yes," he managed, "an Irish whiskey. Make that a double." Briggs stepped outside to join the others, feeling he had little choice at that point.

"I've not seen such a conspiratorial gathering since Nixon invited his former aides to San Clemente," Briggs stated soto voce, bringing all three around to face him quickly. "Good to see you again, Sir Roger," Briggs continued, nodding to the M.P., "and, of course, to see you, princess." He directed the latter comment to Sylvia, wanting to bite his tongue as soon as the words left his mouth, but the old wounds were still fresh. He forged on, joining them at the far end of the patio.

"And I mustn't forget our host. How are you, Howard, and why has it taken so long for you to include me in a purely social event?" He paused dramatically. "Surely, this isn't a business dinner, is it?" he asked with exaggerated innocence.

"Good evening, Donald," Rudyard Howard greeted him, coming forward to extend a hand that was only reluctantly shaken by his guest. "Please join us in a drink before dinner." He had decided to ignore Briggs' sarcastic comments.

"I have one on the way," Briggs told him. "Your lovely wife, Marta—and she is just lovely, you're a lucky man—has taken my order already. I suspect that the question isn't what you can do for me, but what I can do for you. And the answer, whatever the question, is no. You gave your word, and I'm holding you to it."

Before the conversation—or more accurately, confrontation—could go further, Marta Howard appeared with a double Irish whiskey. Sir Roger took advantage of the distraction to redirect the flow of dialogue. If Briggs were to be convinced to involve himself in the matter at hand, he would have to be approached gradually.

"Briggs, my boy, you are looking fit indeed," he said with gusto. "What, have you taken up jogging? It's quite the rage in Britain, you know, and I understand it to be even more so here in the States. Don't you think he looks well, Sylvia?"

"He hasn't changed one bit," she responded, taking a few, casual steps toward Briggs. She looked him up and down, from the top of his head, down across wide shoulders, trim waist and hips, all the way to his feet, with marked deliberation. Her appraisal made Briggs nervous; Sylvia could make him feel like a lad on his first date with just a look.

"When Sylvia and I decided to come to the States for a visit, we knew we simply had to see you again," Sir Roger went on, lying easily now. "The Popov matter brought us all so close together, and it would have been like ignoring a dear relative not to spend some time with you."

Briggs was regaining his shaken equilibrium, however, and turned to Marta Howard to ask the obvious.

"When you called, why didn't you tell me that Sir Roger and Sylvia—Lady Sylvia—would be here?"

"We wanted it be a surprise," Marta said simply. "And it obviously has been. Now, if none of you has an objection, cook informs me that

dinner is ready, and our places are set over there"
—she pointed to the other side of the patio, to a
modest, candle-lit table—"so will you all join us,
please?"

Dinner was leisurely and delicious: fresh salad
greens from Marta's own, small garden, chicken
cordon bleu, pears in wine with whipped cream,
accompanied by a light, white wine. The conversation, if trivial, was pleasant, covering the lighter
range of subjects, from changing fall fashions to
conjecture over the threatened NFL strike. Briggs
was beginning to feel the fool for his suspicions,
and particularly for his remarks when he first
arrived. He and Sylvia had managed to converse
amiably; could it be that she had forgotten?

As the last rays of the setting sun flickered
behind the westward trees and long shadows
enveloped the lawn and house, Howard suggested
that the men retire to his study for drinks. Briggs'
ears tingled; maybe he was right in the first place.
Maybe they wanted something more than friendship from him . . . again. He glanced at Sylvia,
who suddenly could not meet his gaze and excused
herself to accompany Marta to some unnamed,
mysterious place where women disappeared to
when men wanted to talk privately. There was
little else to do, then, but follow Howard and Sir
Roger to the study and find out what they were
scheming.

"I feel a bit uneasy," Sir Roger began as soon
as the study door had been closed behind them,
"after assuring you that we simply wanted to
renew old acquaintances tonight, Briggs—though

it *is* good to see you looking so well. There is a matter of grave importance that we wish to discuss with you.''

"No," Briggs stated flatly, adding defiantly, "you may call me Donald."

"At least hear us out," Howard told him. "We're fully aware of the guarantees extended to you, and we will not violate them."

"He's right, Donald," Sir Roger assured. "Let us give you some background, then you decide if you want to be involved and to what extent. No pressures will be applied. You forget," he smiled, "we gave up all our high cards as your reward for Popov. We *can't* force you to do anything you do not wish to do."

"In that case," replied Briggs, "pour me a whiskey and I'll listen." He plopped himself into the most comfortable chair in the room, a room designed for utility rather than comfort, and gestured for Sir Roger and Howard to do likewise. "But I'll only listen. I won't promise anything more."

Howard poured whiskey for all three of them, then pulled two chairs into the vicinity of his own, which was occupied by Briggs, and opened the discussion.

"Are you familiar with the name Ilya Alexandrovich Gamov?"

Briggs shrugged. "I've heard it. Evening news, I believe. Some big man at the Kremlin, isn't he?" He sipped his whiskey. At least Howard had good taste in booze; it was smooth and warming, expensive stuff.

39

"He's up there," Howard confirmed. "Just behind Andropov and Brezhnev in terms of power and influence. And he's determined to push himself into Andropov's place in the line."

"He's ambitious. That's not unusual, here or there."

"Gamov is Brezhnev's protégé. Old Leonid has a doting father's affection for the man, he can do no wrong and all that. It would appear from the reports we've received that Gamov is amassing power by blackmailing the top men in the Politburo, the military and the KGB." Howard paused, then added, "He may already have the backing he needs to succeed Andropov. No one can take this information to Brezhnev, since Gamov could simply turn it to his own benefit and come off looking better in the old man's eyes."

"If Brezhnev were informed of the blackmailing," Sir Roger interjected in unnecessary explanation, "Gamov would simply turn over the evidence he's collected, claim to be the only incorruptible watchdog of the Revolution, and assure himself Brezhnev's position. Either way, he wins."

"It seems there are a great many powerful people in the Soviet Union who should have listened to Will Rogers," Briggs noted, sipping again at the whiskey. "Didn't he once say something about living one's life so that no harm would be suffered if the town gossip got hold of one's diary?"

"There's more." Howard's face was grim. "Gamov is not sane. He's the hardest line hawk in

40

a flock of them. We know he's conducting some type of work at the Gorky Missile Base, though we haven't been able to break security there and get details. Our fear is that he's priming the military for serious action once he's in power. That's the worst case. At the very least, the prospects for any semblance of nuclear arms limitations—equilateral limitations—would be extinguished with him in power.''

"He's a dangerous man," Sir Roger added.

"And you want me to assassinate him," Briggs concluded.

"Wrong." Howard took pleasure in the look of surprise that crossed Briggs' face. "Andropov has the most to lose as a result of Gamov's black-mailing to gain support, and Andropov would be blamed for Gamov's death. The succession would be up for grabs. I'm not saying that Andropov is any less dedicated a Communist than any other possible successor, but he is a known factor, one we can deal with. We want Andropov to succeed Brezhnev.''

"Then you've lost me," Briggs admitted. "I don't see any options other than to get rid of Gamov, or sit back and take our chances.''

"There is one other alternative." It was Sir Roger's turn to present their case. "We could blacken him with Brezhnev. Pin something so outrageous on him that even his mentor could not fail to either banish or—preferably—execute him.''

"What have you got on him?"

Sir Roger's shoulders slumped noticeably.

41

"Nothing. This would require a frame-up, as they say here in the States, an air-tight fabrication."

Briggs whistled long and low. "If you're looking for ideas on what to nail him with, I'm trapped. If you already have a plan—and I suspect you do—let's hear it."

The ball was back in Howard's court.

"We have a plan, yes, although it must remain pliable to accommodate changing circumstance. In brief, we believe that nothing short of an assassination attempt against Brezhnev that could be quickly, clearly and inalienably linked to Gamov is the only means of accomplishing our aim without sacrificing Andropov."

"Sorry," Briggs broke in. "I'm not going to sacrifice myself by attempting to assassinate Brezhnev and then name Gamov as my superior." He stood, ready to leave. "I have no death wish. If I did, I never would have come back from the first—and last—mission for you."

"Sit down, O'Meara," Howard snapped, becoming irritated. "We never considered asking that of you. We have a number of people inside the Soviet Union who can perform this function. Given the right direction, they should succeed. The key is just that: getting them the direction they need to carry through for us.

"We need a man on the inside, someone who can help them set the details of the plan, oversee it, then leave. Nothing more." Howard stared hard at Briggs, trying in vain to read the thoughts racing behind his noncommittal expression.

"I, direct a bit of action, then out?" Briggs was

skeptical. "What else? Where's the catch?"

"Well," Howard paused, then admitted, "it would be most helpful if you could secure more information about Gamov's dealings at the Gorky Missile Base. But only if circumstances allow."

" 'If *you* could,' " Briggs echoed. "Suddenly we go from speaking in general terms about the need for a director of this group inside Russia, to placing me inside Russia. That's a leap of great faith or total lunacy. I've committed to nothing. You're lucky I'm still even listening."

"There is no one else who can do the job," Sir Roger broke in, imploringly. "You have the background, the tradecraft, and most important, an incredible expertise in the language and an ability to think on your feet, as they say. There is no comparison between this matter and the Popov affair. *You* literally can go in, get the job done and come right out. No one else can do it."

"What's wrong with using some of the CIA agents already there?" Briggs thought this an obvious question, and wondered why that aspect hadn't been already covered.

"Lack of flexibility," Howard responded. "Our own personnel are locked into positions with our ambassadorial delegation or the news services. They have high profiles. They are watched too carefully." He gestured with his massive hands in a movement akin to an umpire calling a strike. "The stringers and informants have much the same problem, and that's compounded by their cultural background, simply the way Russians think. We need a con man. These people are so

43

structured, we can't rely on any of them to pull off a dupe, much less conceive of believable bull on the spur of the moment.''

''I don't know whether to consider that a compliment or a slur,'' Briggs remarked. ''You've both said 'In, do the job, out.' How much of that is bull? Do you have a workable scheme to get me out, or am I to be dumped as I was before?''

Sir Roger didn't miss the change reflected in Briggs' comment when he used the word ''me'' in connection with the operation. He moved quickly to reassure Briggs.

''There is, absolutely, a means to get you back out, and an excellent one. The only reservation we had about sending anyone else in was that no one else can keep such a low profile—blend in, so to speak. Our problem then is that the man is picked off before the plan to retrieve him can be implemented. With you involved, the plan will work.''

''And what, precisely, is the plan?'' Briggs finished his drink and set the empty glass on the floor, next to his chair.

''Sorry,'' Howard told him. ''Not without a commitment from you to take this assignment.''

''That's what I thought.'' Briggs stood and took a few steps toward the door. ''It was a delicious meal—please convey my thanks to Mrs. Howard—and it was most enjoyable seeing you again, Sir Roger. I'm afraid the after-dinner talk has become rather tedious, and I have other matters to attend to.''

''Briggs!'' Sir Roger called out as Briggs reached the door. ''I mean it. The plan is completely feasible. This is not some kind of kamikaze mission, I swear it. I swear it by my late wife's soul.''

Briggs stopped in the open doorway at that, and turned to Sir Roger, moved by the man's oath.

"I'll believe you, Sir Roger," he said, "but I can't give you an answer just yet. I have to think about it."

"Time is of the essence, O'Meara," Howard called after him as he strode down the hall toward the front door.

"I'll let you know in a day or two," Briggs shouted back without turning in Howard's direction, then let himself out and headed toward his car.

Sylvia Hume's appearance at the passenger side of the Porsche just as he slipped the auto into first gear to leave was more than a surprise—Briggs was shocked. She knocked on the car window with open palms, shouting his name and trotting to stay even with the slowly moving vehicle. He hit the brakes, put the car in neutral and unlocked the door for her.

"You weren't going to leave without saying goodbye to me, were you?" she asked, rather breathless, climbing in next to him.

"Well, uh, no . . ." he trailed his words, feeling ridiculous.

"But you're leaving now, aren't you?" she went on, not waiting for a response. "We'll simply have to arrange some other time for a visit, won't we? Perhaps you could show me about the capital."

He was stunned. It was happening again. Or

45

was she part of the softening up committee? He looked out the driver's window at the darkness, then back at her.

"Well?" she prodded.

"Dinner?" he asked. "Tomorrow?"

"Sounds lovely. Where shall we be dining?"

His mind blanked, then groped and came up with a perfect spot.

"L'Auberge Chez Francois," he told her. "It's not far from here, in fact. French Provincial. You'll like it."

"I'll see you here about seven then," she said, and before he knew what had happened, she had hopped from the car and was running back into the house.

"Christ," he said to himself as he moved the Porsche down the drive toward the Pike.

THREE

Briggs had checked himself carefully in the mirror before leaving his apartment. His full head of brown hair, worn in much the same style as John Kennedy chose, had just been shampooed and blown dry, and didn't want to settle into place. Otherwise, he was pleased. He was lean and trim, with only a slight hint noticeable when fully clothed of the strength of which his body was capable. Not bad for a man of forty, he mused, then caught his own reference to age. That was the problem with seeing a woman so much younger than oneself, whether it was Sylvia or any other sweet thing under thirty. It made one conscious of one's own rapidly advancing middle age. He had shrugged it off, though. He didn't dare place too much hope in this evening.

Sylvia had been waiting for him on the porch of the Howard home, wearing a simple yet well-made dress, wrapped against the evening chill in a shawl that Briggs suspected belonged to Marta Howard. It looked good on Sylvia, but seemed familiar. She had skipped down the steps and gotten into the Porsche before he could get out. He didn't mind; the less seen of Sir Roger and Howard tonight, the better.

It took less than a half hour to drive to L'Auberge Chez Francois—simply Chez Francois locally—and Sylvia was duly impressed with the scenery as they twisted and turned through heavy woods crosscut with meandering streams. He had been able to get reservations, nothing short of a miracle. He kept his fingers crossed mentally en route that no errors had taken place, that the reservation would be honored, that their table would be ready. It was important that everything go well this evening.

"Oh, Briggs, this is lovely," Sylvia murmured as they walked into the restaurant. It was a perfect replica of a French provincial inn, rustic yet elegant. Yes, of course, Mr. O'Meara's reservation for 7:00 p.m.; his table was ready, near the fireplace. Briggs had impressed more than a fair share of women with dinner at Chez Francois, but all that was faded glory. Sylvia was impressed. She smiled at him and lightly touched his hand as he held her chair for her.

"I'm so happy we were able to have an evening for ourselves," she told him after their drinks had been served and their dinners ordered. "We seemed to get off on the wrong foot last year, and never properly mended that." She sipped her dry

48

sherry; typically British, she was already set in that habit and loath to digress even in the face of better cuisine. "I do want to apologize for the often horrid way in which I treated you in the past."

"Let's put the past entirely behind us," he responded, not entirely sure what she meant. My God, you're a beautiful woman, he wanted to say. She reached out and touched his hand again, and if the earlier touch were accidental, this one was not.

"Perhaps the problem before was that Father or Uncle Rudy were about, pressuring you and, believe it or not, putting pressure on me," she continued, obviously unwilling to bury their bones without an autopsy. "When my father becomes involved in one of these dangerous, terribly important matters, I come under a great deal of pressure. He's all I have left, you know, so very dear to me, and I worry about him. When these matters of state go poorly, he's up all hours, tense, not eating properly, putting himself under tremendous strain."

A light began to dawn on Briggs, and he worded his next statement carefully.

"Then I would suppose a certain amount of pressure exists now for you, since Sir Roger has been placed in the uncomfortable position of trying to convince me to undertake another mission."

"That's true," she admitted. "I cannot imagine who can be found to measure up to their needs if you decide against it. That will bring so much strain to bear on Father. He's placed all his hopes in you."

"And in you being able to put your feminine wiles to good use for him," Briggs said evenly, bitterly. "Did he authorize you to sleep with me again if need be?"

"That's a filthy accusation!" Sylvia exclaimed. Her face reddened with outrage. Diners at nearby tables turned to look at her, but she didn't notice. "I am here entirely on my own. My father does not direct my actions, and I don't ask him for the authority to eat, sleep or anything else with whomever I choose." Her anger left her less than articulate, but she made up for that in volume.

Briggs leaned toward her, keeping his voice low. "I don't believe you, princess. You're here tonight to convince me to take the mission." He sat back again, and stared at her for several long moments. She was so beautiful. But after the Popov affair, after he had seen her, and they had made love, he had known it would never work out between them. She was the rich, pampered kid from British society, while he was the poor boy from the wrong side of the tracks. She was refined, he was rough; she was cultured, he was a murderer. When they had parted, she had hated him. She had screamed at him, telling him she would never forget the humiliation he had put her through.

He got up. "It's time for me to leave."

"Then go," she snapped. Her teeth were clenched so tightly that it was difficult to understand her words.

"Would you like a ride back to Uncle Rudy's, or would you prefer to stay for your dinner?" Briggs stood next to the table.

"I'll call Uncle Rudy myself, for a car, you twit," she said. She put her head in one hand, braced her elbow on the table and kept her eyes fixed on her sherry glass. "Just get out of my sight. You're despicable. I shall never again attempt to be civil with the likes of you."

Briggs left her sitting there, paid the maitre d', made a quick call to the Howard home to order up a ride for Sylvia, then stopped back at her table. But she refused to acknowledge his presence.

"So that you don't have to return empty-handed, tell them to pick me up at my flat at 8:00 a.m. on Monday. I've decided to take the mission."

Sylvia snapped to attention as he turned quickly to leave.

"Tomorrow, Briggs," she called out. "Not Monday. At 6:00 in the morning. Be ready."

He was anything but ready when the knock came at his door, promptly at 6:00 a.m., and anything but prepared for the identity of his caller.

"Lord love a duck, it's Chiles!" he exclaimed when he opened the door, wearing a brief robe to maintain modesty. "You don't mean to tell me they've still got you playing fetch. I thought by now you'd have nailed down some ambassadorial post at the Court of St. James."

Briggs and Bob Chiles had met before Briggs went on the Popov mission, and had not hit it off all too well at first. Not that one could blame Chiles. It's difficult to start off liking a man who introduces himself by hurling an automobile's alternator at one. Chiles had been that one, and

51

Briggs' aim had been accurate. The two had had some tense moments subsequent to that introduction, but had succeeded in mending their differences.

"I'm still doing the odd jobs," Chiles told him, coming into the apartment when Briggs stepped back as if inviting him to do so. "And you're my odd job for today. Where are your things? Aren't you packed?" He looked around the small, tastefully-furnished living room. "You still need our men to pack a bag for you?" he asked, grinning.

"I've not had much notice of this, you know," Briggs countered, "but I am half packed. Just let me finish and dress." He started toward the bedroom, mumbling, "I must be half packed to take this on again," then shouted loudly enough for Chiles, "Help yourself to some juice or booze or whatever out there."

Briggs was as efficient as the State Department men who had packed for him the last time he'd undertaken a job for their intelligence branch. He was back, dressed and packed, before Chiles had finished a small glass of orange juice. Chiles poured the remainder down the drain; it would spoil in the refrigerator before Briggs returned.

"I assume we're off to the training center," Briggs remarked as they drove the Georgetown Pike to Route 7, then headed west. "But I can't imagine why I have to be run through the course out there again. Perhaps we could stop in and have a tour of Harper's Ferry. I've been meaning to get there, and we go so nearby."

"Forget it," Chiles chuckled. "We're on a tight

schedule. And if you're thinking that you can get me to give you some kind of information on your training, you're off base. I don't know what kind of training you'll be getting. Just wait and see."

The route to the training center, winding into the Blue Ridge Mountains, was familiar to Briggs, though he'd only traveled it once before. Chiles cut away from the main road southeast of Harper's Ferry, winding into heavily-forested land, until they came to the secluded training center, a three-story building with a false front and long porch. Other, smaller buildings were clustered around it; off in the distance, he could see the obstacle course, where he had finally settled his differences with Chiles.

Burt Higgins greeted them both when they went to administration, on the first floor of the main building, to sign in. He seemed genuinely pleased to see Briggs again. Higgins' eyes were protruding even more than usual, and several strands of wispy, white hair at the top of his head swayed to and fro as he gestured and spoke.

"O'Meara, it's a pleasure, a genuine pleasure, to have you back here again." He extended his hand, and Briggs shook it. "You were my quickest study, quickest temper, too. Come, get yourself settled in your room first . . . where have they got you, second floor, yes, second floor, and then meet me back in the dining hall."

"Look, Higgins," Briggs interrupted, "I just want to make it perfectly clear that I'm not going through all that same crap I had to go through last year. Especially the medicos and the shrinks. I still don't want to screw my mother, so not much has changed."

"No problem," Higgins assured him. "We didn't even have that in mind this time. See you later." He patted him on the back and left.

Briggs wasn't surprised to find Howard and Sir Roger waiting along with Burt Higgins when he came back from his room some fifteen minutes later. In fact, he'd been surprised not to have spotted them on the road on the way there.

"I suppose you'll share your great plan with me, gentlemen," Briggs said, joining them at a secluded end of the dining hall. "No need to candy it up by having a pretty, young woman slip it to me." It gave him satisfaction to see Sir Roger wince at the remark.

"Look, Briggs, I had nothing to do with Sylvia's ploy. Had I known about it, I would have stopped her. I don't work that way," Sir Roger said.

"I do," Howard told him bluntly. "She wanted to see you, alone, and since she had already made a dinner date with you, I asked her to exert her influence. Now, can we get down to business?"

"Be my guest." Briggs was indifferent, at least on the outside. On the inside, he was pleased to know that Sylvia had approached him and invited him to dinner on her own. He was also alert as the details of his mission were presented to him, in contrast to his exterior attitude. His life could depend upon it.

"We have contacts for you in Moscow, and a means of entry and exit. First, the entry."

Howard opened a detailed map of the western half of the Soviet Union and pointed with the end of a pencil toward the Finnish border. "You'll come in here, near Vyborg, from Finland. No matter which way we look at this, it's the best entry point in terms of getting across the border itself with the least risk, and then getting to Moscow.

"From Vyborg, you'll travel by train to Leningrad, and then from Leningrad to Moscow, by commercial carrier, an Aeroflot interior flight. We even have you booked on it." Howard smiled slightly at the level of efficiency his organization could achieve.

"Your cover during this phase will be as a mid-level bureaucrat with the KGB, returning from a brief holiday in Finland. We've got all your papers in order, clothing, luggage, all the details, as usual, and have seen to all the fine points on them. By that, I mean that the cut of the clothing, the labels, the paraphernalia are all correct for a man of such occupation. Our tailor will be by shortly to make certain your dimensions haven't changed with the good life you've been leading."

"Keep talking," Briggs instructed, looking bored, but listening intently.

"When you get to Moscow, you are to contact our group there. You'll have to use extreme care in this. Although we believe we've given you an excellent cover, you never know when you might be followed, so watch out for that. If you're followed, ditch them, any way you have to. We can't expose our people. If we do, the entire mission could be lost.

"This fellow," Howard pulled an eight-by-ten glossy photograph from a manila envelope, "is head of our group. Do you recognize him?"

Briggs studied the picture, showing a man in his thirties, bearded, long haired, with earlocks worn in the Hasidic tradition. His eyes seemed to burn through him, even from a photo.

"Goetz Solchek, the Nobel Prize winner for literature a few years ago. I always wanted to make his novel, *Frozen In Hell,* into a movie. Of course," he shrugged, "that was another world ago. You mean he's an agent?"

"No, he's not an agent. He's not even a stringer," Howard clarified. "He's a dissident with strong, if not fanatic, anti-Soviet feelings. As you know, he's been refused permission to emigrate to Israel, his words have been banned, and he's chafing badly under the pressure."

"Now you can see why it is imperative that you not be followed when you leave the airport at Moscow," Sir Roger pointed out. "This fellow must be protected—cultivated."

"He has a group of others, I take it?" probed Briggs. "I assume some of them are professionals."

"He has a group, right, of other dissidents. No pros. Sorry, but I'm afraid that's the best we could do this time around." Howard could understand Briggs' reluctance to be thrust into a group of amateur spies in the Russian capital. "We believe that their abilities will be more than sufficient, however; that, and their contacts. You will work Slochek and his people to conceive of and let them carry out a faked assassination attempt against the premier."

"Give me some details on that." Briggs no longer maintained his look of indifference.

"I wish I had some. That's why we need you there. You will have to trail the premier, determine weak points where such an attempt may be staged, select the individual who will carry it out, and make certain that all roads, so to speak, lead back to Gamov. That is your primary mission."

"And then I leave? How do I get out?"

"Not so fast," Sir Roger interjected. "There is a secondary mission here, to be carried out if you—in your sole discretion—think that it can be done. If possible, we would like you to get inside the Gorky Missile Base and ascertain what it is Gamov is up to there."

"That's a suicide mission!"

"Not necessarily," Sir Roger said calmly. "To facilitate access to the missile base, we will provide you with the identity and uniform of a ranking Polish officer. The cover would be that you are there to participate in training and then return to Poland. No one will think it strange when, after a bit, you don't return; it will be assumed that your training was completed."

"I don't know . . ." Briggs' words trailed off.

"Of course, you don't know, old chap. That's why this phase is left to your sole discretion. But the papers and uniform will be at the British Embassy, with one of my people—and only one—ready to hand them over to you. No decision is required, or even possible, at this point. If you come by to see Phil Smythe, you will have decided to attempt it, and he will provide you with whatever you need. Everything will be transported in by diplomatic pouch before you ever leave the training center."

"And? When do we get to the part about getting out of the country?"

"We've got that covered, too." It was Howard's turn again. He directed attention to the map, pointing once more to the area along the Finnish border. "We have your transportation out, waiting for you, already. You'll be flying out via jet—small jet, I'm afraid, but fast enough for our purposes. It's concealed near Lake Onega, here." He pointed with his pencil tip, leaving a small dot in his wake on the map, not far from Petrozavodsk. "You'll be out in a matter of minutes, before they even realize their air space has been breached."

"Who's my pilot," asked Briggs, "another dissident?"

"You are." Howard kept the statement simple so that it could sink in. It didn't take long.

"You really are insane, Howard. I can't fly a damned plane. Christ, I can't even hang glide. Forget it. It's scrapped. I'm not going to do it."

"Why do you think you're here?" It was the first Burt Higgins had spoken during the briefing. "This is a training center, and we're going to train you to fly a plane."

"It's crazy," Briggs reiterated, but with less force. At the back of his mind, a thought was knocking: Maybe it would work.

"We realize that piloting a jet will be new for you, even with intensive training." Howard took the floor again. "That was a factor in choosing this particular area to secrete the plane for your use—that, and the proximity to the border. By the time you are ready to leave, Briggs, Lake Onega will be frozen solidly enough to take the weight of the jet, but the snow should not be too deep yet. You'll be able to taxi out onto the lake and use it as a runway."

"A very long runway," Higgins added. "Our experts tell us that inexperienced pilots have their greatest difficulty with takeoff because they tend to use up more runway than they have. You won't run off the end on Lake Onega."

Briggs sat quietly for a full moment, thinking. It was nuts, the whole venture, but he'd already committed to at least the first phase of it, contacting and assisting Slochek and his group. What the hell, if he lived through it, knowing how to fly could come in handy.

"Two questions," he said. "First, will I have a leg up on getting a pilot's license when I get back?"

"I imagine that could be arranged." Howard held back a chuckle. O'Meara could be so exasperating, so rude, then turn around and crack jokes that even a dour man such as he could not resist.

"And second, when do we start the pilot training?"

"At two o'clock," Burt Higgins answered, "which is only three hours away. I suggest that we allow Mr. O'Meara the opportunity to visit our tailor and Wyatt in the meantime.''

"Wait a minute." Briggs held up his hand, signalling abeyance. "No need for me to see Wyatt. I'm not carrying any guns, not using any guns. I have all I need." He reached behind his back to his waistband and drew the stiletto. A random ray of sunlight caught the blade and flashed at the group.

"Think of Wyatt as an airline stewardess, instead of an armorer. The stewardess must offer you refreshments and assistance as part of her job. Wyatt must offer you armaments as part of his job. You are obliged to accept neither." Higgins had a quaint way of making comparisons. Briggs decided to acquiesce.

"Oh, and Briggs," Higgins called out to him as the group dispersed and he headed toward his room, "you'll be pleased to know that an old friend of yours will be instructing you in the cockpit. Our Mr. Danielson. He'll be at the desk to call for you at two sharp."

FOUR

The Link simulator-trainer was located in one of the technical section buildings to the east of the main administration center. The afternoon was quite bright, and still on the warm side when Briggs entered the building where he was greeted with the soft, subdued air of dim red and blue lights, and the muted hush of air conditioning.

Stu Danielson, who doubled here at the school as a confidence course master, as well as the flight-simulator training director, was a tall, very thin man who moved with an economy of motion. He, along with Bob Chiles and a couple of others, had been in on the earlier troubles with Briggs. They had not hit it off at first. But like the others, Danielson turned out to be not so bad after all.

He was waiting just within the simulator main frame area (called the lounge) speaking up at the equipment controller who sat in a booth ten feet above. The hatch to the trainer was open.

"You're going to teach me to fly in that thing?" Briggs asked.

Danielson turned around, a grin spreading over his face. He came over and shook hands. "Either that or kill you trying."

Briggs laughed. "Good to see you again, Stu. Although I never thought I'd be back."

"We all figured you'd show up sooner or later."

"You did, did you?"

Danielson nodded, then looked at his watch. "I was just getting ready to come get you. We're a little short on time."

"As usual."

"Yes. From what I understand, you've had no flight training. None?"

"Not a bit."

Danielson looked glum. "Then let's get started." He led Briggs over to the simulator and helped him climb up and strap into the bucket seat.

"I'm not going to bore you with a lot of theory. That can come later when you return. For now I'm just going to teach you the switches, the instruments and the physical motions you're going to have to go through to get the bird off the ice, over the border and back down again. You won't be near any airports, so you won't have to worry about lining up with runways, or with other traffic. Just up, over and down."

Briggs had been studying the instrument panel of the trainer. The labels were all in Russian.

Straightforward. Air speed indicator, rate of climb, turn and bank, artificial horizon, turbine rpms, fuel consumption and tankage management, oxygen, and temperature, as well as the electronics—among them radios, navigation equipment, radar and fire control systems for the ship's weapons.

"This the plane I'll be flying?"

"The panel is very similar," Danielson said at his shoulder. "You'll be flying a MiG-21UTI, the trainer version of the old MiG-21.

"I thought this was supposed to be a slow plane?"

"It is," Danielson said. "Relatively speaking."

Briggs' eyes narrowed. "They'll be expecting me?"

"No telling. But you'll be lifting off from the north end of Lake Onega. The Petrozavodsk Military Area Command Base is located at the south side of the lake. Barely fifty miles away."

"Faster MiGs?"

"Surface-to-air missiles, I'm told."

Briggs turned his attention back to the panel. "How far to the Finnish border?"

"Just about 125 air miles."

"I'll have to get it right the first time. No mistakes."

"Something like that. As soon as you're airborne, the Finnish Perimeter Radar Service will be notified."

Briggs had to smile. "And the Finns will send up their air force to hold off the bad Russians."

"Nope. But they won't shoot you down . . . we

don't think."

Danielson stepped back on the platform and closed the hatch as Briggs donned the helmet with its built-in microphone and earphones. The simulator controller's voice came through, soft, even and very assured.

"Good afternoon Commander O'Meara. We will begin with our instrument and controls identification and function check list."

A light snow was falling when a black Zil limousine glided into the courtyard of the All-Union Hospital just off Vosstaniya and continued around to a rear entryway. Four military jeeps, each with four heavily-armed soldiers, were already there, and in the distance from the northwest came the heavy chop of an approaching helicopter.

The man next to the driver in the Zil raised a walkie-talkie to his lips and keyed the microphone. "Morning Glory, this is Transport One. In place."

"Where is Unit Two?" the speaker crackled at the same moment a second limousine pulled up.

"Just arrived. Air One is coming in as well."

There was a moment of silence. "On our way."

Blinov and the driver, Matushin, got out of the Zil, hurried up to the jeeps, where they spoke with the drivers, then stationed themselves at the hospital door.

The helicopter's landing lights came on moments later, and the big machine came noisily in for a landing fifty yards away in the parking lot, its rotors slowing but not stopping.

The jeeps were started, their lights on.

Blinov raised the walkie-talkie. "Ready for exit," he said softly.

"Coming out," came the reply.

Blinov pocketed the radio, then turned and opened the hospital door as two large men helped a third outside, across the walk, and over to the first limousine.

Blinov hurried ahead to open the rear door, then stood back as Fedorov and Tikhvinsky helped Comrade Party Secretary Leonid Brezhnev into the car.

When he was settled inside, the other two men, who closely resembled him, took off in different directions—one across to the helicopter, the other to the limousine at the rear.

Within a couple of minutes the helicopter had lifted off and the second limousine, followed by all four jeeps had departed.

Blinov's heart was hammering. This was the second time this month that his unit had gotten *the* detail. He didn't want to believe these precautions were necessary. There were no gangsters here in Moscow like there were in New York. Yet someone—perhaps Comrade Brezhnev himself—had thought a danger existed.

"We're away," the walkie-talkie hissed.

Blinov raised it to his lips as Matushin put the car in gear and headed away from the hospital. "En route," he said, then put the radio beside him on the seat.

For the past half dozen months the security procedures around Brezhnev had been stringently tightened. There had been a lot of talk about the old man. Not just assassination rumors, but health stories. Brezhnev was failing. It was only a matter of time before he was dead. One of the grim jokes going around Moscow was about the assassin who was hired to kill Brezhnev, but had to return his fee because the old man had died of fright when he showed up.

Those were jokes. Nothing to take seriously. Moscow had always been filled with gallows humor. It meant nothing.

But helicopters, and second limousines with look-alikes, were serious to Blinov's way of thinking.

Once clear of the hospital, Matushin headed back toward Red Square, from where he drove out to Kutuzovsky Prospekt where Brezhnev's apartment was located.

As he had on the other evenings he had pulled this detail, Blinov held himself erect in his seat, but his eyes kept moving as he surveyed the streets and buildings they passed.

Two blocks from the apartment, Matushin slowed down, his hands tightly gripping the steering wheel.

Blinov's gut was aching. A dozen scenarios, all of them gruesome, flashed through his mind. A single car. Two bodyguards. They were sitting ducks.

Across the last intersection, Blinov could see the guardhouse in front of Brezhnev's building.

Nothing seemed out of the ordinary. In fact, the sudden thought came to him, everything seemed just a little *too* quiet.

He started to turn, when the man in the back seat pulled off his thick fur hat, unwound his wool scarf and unbuttoned his overcoat. "He's safe."

Blinov jerked the rest of the way around. "Fedorov!"

The man grunted. "You may take me home, or back to the Center."

Matushin was looking in the rear view mirror. He was shaking his head. He too had been taken in. But the relief was sweet, Blinov thought.

A large delivery van careened around the corner and came up behind them, its headlights on high beams.

"Crazy bastard . . ." Matushin started to say as he pulled over, when Blinov and Fedorov both realized at the same moment what was happening.

"Go! Go!" Blinov shouted as he pulled out his automatic.

The van passed them, and its rear doors slammed open to reveal four men in the back, armed with rifles. They opened fire immediately, the shots starring the bulletproof windshield.

Blinov had cranked down his window. He leaned out and began firing rapidly into the back of the van. Fedorov was doing the same from the back seat.

One of the would-be assassins went down, and a second dropped to his knees. But a third man had disappeared inside the van. A moment later he was again at the open door, a large bucket in his hand.

He swung the bucket at the same moment Blinov fired, hitting him in the chest. But it was too late. The liquid that had been in the bucket doused the car. Instantly the smell of gasoline was strong.

"No . . ." Fedorov wailed from the back seat, as Matushin slammed on the brakes and slewed the big limousine around in an attempt to get out of the way.

Blinov kept firing into the back of the truck as one of the terrorists lit a torch and threw it.

Blinov watched in horror as the torch arced up away from the truck, then came down with a heavy thump on the roof of their car, which was turned instantly into an inferno.

It was the evening of the fourth day of his training, and Briggs was about to shut off the light in his room and get a few hours of sleep before his 0100 flight-simulator appointment. He was dead tired, and although he was convinced that he would be able to fly the jet out of there, and more or less land it in one piece across the border in Finland, he wasn't so sure about everything else.

Two things specifically bothered him, and bothered him deeply, although he had not yet mentioned either.

The first was his connection with the Nobel Prize winner Solchek. The man was an avowed anti-communist, and a Jew. He wanted out of the country. Yet if and when Briggs approached him, it would be as an American approaching a Russian . . . a dissident, but a Russian nevertheless.

If anything were to happen, if anything went wrong, and that possibility certainly was not outside the realm of imagination, then it was also likely that the entire operation could blow up in their faces. He could see the Tass headlines now: AMERICAN ASSASSINATION PLOT ON PARTY SECRETARY BREZHNEV FAILS! AMERICAN EXECUTED!

The second problem was Solchek and men like him—more specifically what would happen to him and the others if and when the operation was pulled off.

The assassination attempt was going to have to appear very real, and it had to be traceable back to Gamov.

None of that was really difficult, except for the fact that Solchek, or at least someone from the group was going to have to be caught with the "evidence" of Gamov's complicity.

Someone was going to have to be sacrificed. Whoever it was would have to die before any serious questioning could begin.

Briggs stood by the window, next to the light switch, looking out across the compound. There was some activity this evening over on the small arms range. This place was never completely quiet. Higgins had once explained that only the students are ever allowed to sleep, and then only for a few minutes at a time. It wasn't far from the truth.

How would the sacrificial lamb be selected? Briggs wondered. By lot? Eeny, meeny, miney, moe? Or would Solchek and a dozen like him volunteer.

Briggs had no stomach for that.

Someone knocked at his door. He turned around. "It's open."

Burt Higgins came in, followed by Bob Chiles. Chiles carried a bottle of Irish whiskey and three glasses. They both seemed smugly pleased with themselves.

"Let me guess," Briggs said dryly. "Howard is off base for the evening. Everyone is tickled with my progress. And you two want to have a party."

"Two out of three isn't bad," Chiles said. He handed Briggs a glass, opened the bottle and poured him a stiff shot. He waited until Briggs drank it down, then poured him another. He poured one for Higgins, one for himself then perched on the edge of the bed, the bottle on the floor at his feet.

Briggs leaned against the window frame, and Higgins took up position at the desk.

"Rudy had to return to Washington," Higgins said. "You were right about that."

Something had happened to affect their mission. Briggs could see it written all over their faces.

"The secretary wanted him to tag along up to Camp David," Chiles said. "And yes, everyone is happy with your progress. So happy in fact . . ."

Higgins held him off. "No party though, Donald, just a couple of drinks. You'll be leaving tomorrow."

Briggs stood bolt upright, away from the window. "What?" He wasn't ready by a long shot.

He smile left Higgins' lips. He put his drink

down. "We just received word from our embassy in Moscow that an attempt was made on Brezhnev's life last night."

Briggs held himself very still. "An attempt? It failed?"

"From what we understand. In fact Brezhnev wasn't anywhere near the fray."

"Give it to me one at a time," Briggs said.

"We've known for several months now that Brezhnev has been taking extra precautions with his movements. He doesn't get out in public much, and when he does he's surrounded by bodyguards," Higgins said.

"What we didn't know," Chiles said, "was that Brezhnev has apparently employed at least one double."

"Are we sure?" Briggs asked.

"We weren't until this incident," Chiles said. "But now we are."

"None of this was in *Izvestia?*"

Higgins shook his head. "Not a peep. From what we can gather, Brezhnev was released from the All-Union Hospital where he had been for a couple of days for a checkup. But what none of us knew for sure until later was that Brezhnev evidently went by helicopter to his *dacha* outside the city, while his double headed by limousine back to his apartment."

"The limo was hit?"

"About a half a block from his apartment," Chiles said. "A truck or van came up alongside the limo, there was some gunplay, and then the limo was doused with gasoline and set afire."

"Lordy," Briggs said, wincing.

"Hell of a way to have to go," Chiles agreed.

"The assassins were caught?"

"There were four of them, plus the driver. They all were killed."

Briggs' mind was working fast. "Have any connections been found?"

"It's too early to tell," Higgins said. "Probably just dissidents."

"It'll make my job more difficult," Briggs said half to himself. "Security around Brezhnev will be tighter than ever. His people more jumpy."

"Perfect for a second attempt," Chiles said.

Briggs looked up. "A single assassination attempt could be put down to a dissident group. To a bunch of crazies. But two attempts . . . one right after the other . . . indicates organization."

"Gamov," Higgins said with a smile.

"That part certainly will be a hell of a lot more convincing, won't it?" Briggs said.

"Which is why we have to move now."

"I have a simulator session in a couple of hours."

"I know," Higgins said. "We've already spoken with Danielson. He says you'll be ready."

Briggs grinned. "I'll have to ask him if he'd ride with me."

"We have a military transport for you over to Ramstein Air Base in Germany, first thing in the morning out of Andrews. From there you'll pick up your civilian ID in Kaiserslautern on which you can take a plane up to Helsinki."

"From there?"

"It'll be in your package. You'll cross at Vyborg, by train to Leningrad and from there an internal flight to Moscow. You'll be Petr Nikolai Solkov, a deputy chief in the Second Chief Directorate's 7th Department."

"Tourists," Briggs said.

"Right. You've been on vacation to Finland, but now it's time to get back to work watching all the baddie tourists from the West."

"That's to Moscow. How about when I get there?"

"The same," Higgins said.

"Solchek knows I'm coming, then?"

Higgins nodded.

Briggs started to say that he was having difficulty accepting that last bit of the operation, but then he thought better of it. He did not really want to approach Solchek in that fashion because it entailed too much of an exposure. It was too risky. If he objected now, Howard would come up with something else. By keeping his peace he'd be able to do pretty much as he wanted. If he could figure out another way.

Chiles got up and brought the whiskey over to where Briggs stood, and poured him another. They clicked glasses.

"I'll be over a day later," Chiles said.

"A reception committee?" Briggs asked. "How nice."

"Ilomantsi. It's a little town right on the border directly west of Lake Onega."

Higgins got to his feet. "We're both flying with you to Ramstein in the morning. It'll give us

73

another six or eight hours on your briefing."

"We don't want Brezhnev hurt, but we do want Gamov out of the box?"

"That's right," Higgins said. "Nothing more than that, other than a quick peek at the goings on at Gorky Missile Base if you've the time and you're still in the clear. Your alternate ID will be arranged through our embassy."

"Who will be my contact?"

"We'll have a letter drop set up. I'll brief you on the specifics tomorrow."

Briggs nodded, tiredly. He wanted to get to bed now, although he did not think he would be able to sleep.

At the door Higgins stopped. "You're going to have to carry a gun, you know."

"As Solkov?"

Higgins nodded.

"Doesn't mean I have to use it," Briggs said.

"See you in the morning," Higgins said. Chiles smiled and nodded and they both were gone.

Briggs finished his drink, got undressed, switched off the light and slipped into bed. He closed his eyes and immediately he had a picture of a Hasidic Jew, Solchek, being gunned down by a firing squad in the courtyard of Lubyanka Prison. The man kept shouting that he was innocent . . . that it was the American, but no one was listening to him.

Someone knocked at the door. Briggs groaned and sat up. "It's open, Burt," he snapped. He turned the light on.

The door opened and Sylvia Hume, wearing

blue jeans and a light sweater, came in. She closed the door.

"What the hell are you doing here?" Briggs asked.

She seemed breathless. "They said you'd be leaving in the morning."

"Does your father know you've come here?"

She shook her head. "Do you want me to leave?"

Briggs looked at her, then finally nodded. "Yes," he said, softly. She seemed very disappointed, and she turned away. "What the hell are you doing here?" he asked.

She turned back. "I wanted to see you. There was so much . . . left unresolved . . . the last time."

"This isn't right, you know," Briggs said, trying to be as gentle as possible. "It will not work between us."

She came slowly across the room to his side, and looked down at him. Her eyes were filling.

Briggs shook his head, reached out and shut off the light, then drew her down to him, their lips meeting, a moan coming from deep in her throat.

Then she was taking her clothes off, and they were nude in each other's arms, her breasts crushed against his chest, her long, incredibly soft legs intertwined in his, as he kissed her neck.

"Briggs . . . oh, God . . . Briggs," she breathed. She pulled him over on top of her, and guided him inside, and suddenly they were making love . . . moving together in perfect unison—all thoughts of Gamov, and Brezhnev and the Russian Jew, Solchek, fleeing from Briggs' mind.

FIVE

It was chilly in west central Germany, and Briggs shivered as he climbed out of the military sedan that had brought him to a remote section of Ramstein Air Force Base.

Burt Higgins got out from behind the wheel and walked with Briggs over to the two-year-old Mercedes with German plates parked a few yards away.

"I spoke with Howard just before we came out," Higgins said.

"Everything quiet?"

"More or less. Security around Brezhnev has tightened up. But we expected that."

Briggs looked through the wire mesh fence, and across the narrow road to a dark stand of pine. The wind was raw, the trees would provide shelter. He wished he had never agreed to take another assignment. Yet a part of him was getting the old feeling of looseness. Every muscle in his body seemed like a hydraulic ram—liquid, yet ready at an instant's notice to strike out. A large part of him wanted to return to the States, to his mundane, safe job at state. But another, more intense part of him, was looking forward to whatever might come. It was strange. It felt as if there were several personalities all wrapped up inside his head. On the one hand he was Donald O'Meara, yet he was beginning to feel like Victor Renkin, an American businessman on his way to Finland. Somewhere even deeper was Petr Solkov, a dedicated KGB internal agent.

"There are times when I wonder if I'm sane," he said to Higgins.

"We're in the wrong business for sanity, Briggs, you knew that before you signed on."

Briggs smiled. "Yeah," he said.

"Good luck," Higgins said. They shook hands. Then Briggs got into the Mercedes as Higgins unlocked the gate in the fence and swung it open. Briggs cranked down the window.

"Burt . . . don't be alarmed by whatever you hear," Briggs said as he passed.

"What the hell do you mean by that?" Higgins shouted.

"I may not stick with the scenario," Briggs said as he cleared the fence. He rolled up the window, the last thing he heard Higgins shouting was the word, "bastard," and then he was on his way into Kaiserslautern.

In town, Briggs checked out of the Banhof Hotel (where Higgins, or one of the team over here, had checked him in a couple of days ago) to start his track which would be traceable should anyone check back on him. He then took the E12 Autobahn to Mannheim and from there the 34 the few miles north to the Rhein-Main Airport at Frankfurt, where he turned in his car at the Hertz counter.

"We hope you had a pleasant stay, Mr. Renkin," the girl at the car counter said.

Briggs smiled, and nodded effusively. He had a drink at the *stube* in the terminal and then presented himself to the Lufthansa counter where he picked up his ticket to Helsinki. He chatted amiably with the ticket clerks as he checked his suitcase through, then carried his one small bag across to the waiting area. He struck up a conversation with an American family from Montana on the way to Finland for a vacation. By the time they boarded the plane, they were sick to death of Mr. Renkin and his stupid off-color stories about life as a salesman. But they'd never forget him if someone happened to question them.

On the three hour flight, Briggs bored his seat mate to tears with stories about life in Iowa and Nebraska.

Similarly he irritated the customs agent at Helsinki so badly, the man waved him through after finishing only half his inspection.

He rented a car at the airport and drove up the coast to Kotka, the capital city of the Kymi province, just across the Gulf of Finland from Leningrad. As he drove he could almost feel the hulking presence of the gigantic Soviet Union less than seventy-five miles away. Although the sun was shining from a wonderfully blue sky, the day was very cold—well below freezing—and the nearness of the Soviet Union made it seem even colder.

A few days ago he was in the States. A few hours ago he had been in Germany. In not too many hours he'd be inside Russia once again.

He could vividly remember his days as a young man growing up in London's Soho district. His mother had been brutally murdered by Soviet NKVD or GRU agents after the war because of work his father had been doing. Her death had left him alone, and so he had begun to wander the streets. It was then that the emigré community of Soho—the displaced Russians, Albanians and Bulgarians who had worked for British intelligence during the war—took him in as their adopted son, as their plaything. He went through a very intense period of training then in footwork, in letter drops and codes, in radio work, in all the tradecraft of a good agent. He was also taught the Russian language and ideals, so well that by the time he was in his teens, he could speak, think and certainly pass as a Russian.

It was then he killed his first man under the direction and guidance of his emigré instructors. A Russian airline employee working in London had been identified as an intelligence agent. Briggs set the man up, stalked him, and murdered him without compunction or regrets (those would come later) his task made bearable by the thought of his mother's death at the hands of the Soviets.

As he thought about his job now, it too was made easier, more palatable by the thought of his mother. He had discovered her body in their apartment as a young lad. He had seen with his own eyes the brutal evidence of Soviet tradecraft.

It was well after 6:00 p.m. when Briggs turned his rental car in at the service center downtown, where he had to pay an extra charge to have the car driven back to Helsinki.

From there he took a bus to the railway station where in the men's room he quickly changed his clothes for a thicker, more roughly-cut jacket, baggier trousers and a shapeless shirt and tie. He strapped the big Graz-Buyra on beneath his left arm, then tossed his overcoat over his arm, stuffed his now-empty overnight bag back in the suitcase, and, head held high, chin square, marched briskly outside and down the block to a small, second class hotel.

"Petr Nikolai Solkov," he announced to the desk clerk, slapping his passport down on the counter.

"Good afternoon, sir," the older man said tiredly, in bad Russian. He handed over a pen and a registration card. "Do you wish the room for one night, or for longer?"

"My train leaves in the morning," Briggs said, his Russian hard, precise, obviously Moscow. He filled out the registration card and slammed the pen down. The clerk winced, glanced at the card, then took it and the passport and handed Briggs a key.

"Third floor in the rear."

Briggs nodded, picked up his suitcase, and marched to the stairs and up to his room, not allowing himself to relax out of character until he was safely inside, and the door locked. Then he sighed.

A lot of Russians came into Finland on holiday, so his presence here like this would cause no undue interest. The police would look at his passport this evening, routinely checking to make sure he wasn't on any wanted lists, and then return it before six.

If there were any problems, any whatsoever, they would show up then. The signal would come from Moscow to Washington where it would be relayed to Higgins at the communications center just outside Ramstein. Within minutes—literally—Briggs's Soviet identity could be on the Interpol network: hold for questions—urgent.

He splashed some water on his face, looked in the mirror to make sure he was presentable, and went downstairs where he had his dinner, drinking half a carafe of vodka in the Russian manner. Briggs was partial to Irish whiskey, and hated vodka, but it was part of his cover.

Back in his room he put a few coins in the radio, and laid down on the bed as the music came on. He fell asleep before the metered time ran out.

At the Ramstein weather station Briggs had watched the development of the first major early winter front developing in the Arctic northwest.

When he awoke Wednesday morning, he could hear the wind howling around the back of the hotel. He got up and went to the window.

It was still dark out, but he could see that it was snowing heavily, and it looked very cold and inhospitable out there. He shivered, thinking for the moment of Southern California.

Before Sir Roger and Rudyard Howard had approached him to work for the State Department's intelligence division, he had been more or less happy producing and directing B-movies in Hollywood. At this moment he missed the Southern Californian warmth.

It was well past six by the time he had cleaned up and went downstairs. He had a quick breakfast of smoked salmon, cheese and an orange, along with lemon tea, then went to the desk where he checked out and paid his bill.

The clerk did not hesitate or show any sign that everything wasn't all right as he handed over the passport.

"Have a pleasant journey, Comrade Solkov."

"Da," Briggs said brusquely. He hunched up his overcoat, and went out into the storm.

It was very cold and the wind-driven snow stung his cheeks as he trudged the block up to the train depot. The snowplows were out, road-sanding crew right behind them. Beneath the violet streetlights the scene seemed unreal, almost surreal. But it was something he'd have to get used to over the next days or weeks. Winter came very early to this part of the world.

His reservations were in order and he picked up

his tickets at the counter, then went across to the waiting area, where within a few minutes the gates were opened and the small knot of people were allowed trackside, and aboard the train.

Briggs took a window seat, stowing his suitcase in the overhead rack, then lit a Turkish cigarette and settled back for the four-and-a-half-hour trip to Leningrad.

Someone was playing music from a radio, and Briggs could smell the odors of smoked fish and sausage. These were all Russians aboard this train. Returning from holidays or business trips. Now that they were on their way home, they had become practical again . . . eating a picnic lunch instead of spending their money in the dining car.

The day coach was less than half full when the train started out of the station, and the conductor started through collecting tickets. Briggs' heart lurched a little as he prepared himself for a return to the Soviet Union.

Away from the station they headed north out of the city along the seashore. As the dawn finally came Briggs could see large waves, their white breaking crests disappearing into the snowstorm. An overwhelming sense of loneliness came over him at that moment, and he looked away from the window.

A lot of the people in the day coach were traveling together. Families, friends, lovers, business partners.

But he had no one. The one woman on this Earth he loved was denied any life with him because of the difference in their histories, and because of the nature of his work.

Briggs had always been a loner. But at this moment he was lonely too.

Brezhnev's dacha was located twenty-five miles north of Moscow in a thick stand of birch. In the old days, the place had been little more than a lovely large house in the woods. A hunting retreat for one of the Czar's family. Ever since Camp David, however, the place had been transformed into a compound (as yet unnamed), complete with tall fences, guards and guard towers, roving patrols, and at least a dozen buildings housing everything from mess halls and baracks for the guards, to a complete radio and television studio, a small theater and a very complete library. If the American president could have such a place, then the leader of the Soviet Union certainly could as well.

It was to this place that Ilya Gamov came, like a wolf scouting out the lair he meant to make his. They came to the main highway, which was Dmitrovskoye Road, and Gamov lowered the privacy screen that separated the rear seat area of his limousine from the front and leaned forward.

"Pull over here," he said gently. His aide, Reza Makat was driving. He slowed the big car and pulled it over to the side of the road.

Gamov let himself out of the car, and slowly walked around to the front, and a few yards beyond. He raised his head and sniffed the air, then looked toward the west. A few light snow flakes were falling, and the gentle wind had begun to back to the northwest. A storm was coming. But there was something else. Something almost indefinable, at the very edge even of Gamov's powerful intuition.

He turned the rest of the way around so that he was facing west, and the feeling grew stronger. Alarm. Trouble. He felt like a divining rod being drawn to troubled waters.

Reza had gotten out of the car, and his shoes crunched on the gravel at the side of the road as he came forward.

Gamov glanced at him. "Do you feel it, Reza my old friend?"

Reza peered toward the forests to the west, his face to the west wind. He shrugged. "A storm is developing from Finland. It will reach us."

"Yes, but it's more than that. Can't you feel it?"

Reza looked at Gamov and shook his head. But he did feel something. Not from the west, as Gamov indicated, but from Gamov himself. It was as if Reza were watching a volcano ready to explode at any moment. A powerful vibration emanated from him.

"I do," Gamov said after a moment of silence. He turned and strode back to the limousine where he climbed in and slammed the door.

Reza climbed behind the wheel, and they drove the rest of the way out to the first secretary's dacha in silence.

They were stopped at the main gate, but were waved through as soon as Gamov was recognized.

A long, wide drive wound its way up a small hill, then down the other side into a long, gently-sloping valley, at the bottom of which was Brezhnev's dacha, rising like some sort of haphazard pile next to a wide creek—frozen now at this time of the year.

A second set of guards were waiting for them when they reached the house. One of the housemen crisply opened the limousine's rear door, then stepped aside as Gamov got out, rose to his full, impressive height, and, carrying his thick briefcase, strode up the stairs and into the huge house.

Inside he and his briefcase were secretly X-rayed, although Gamov knew about it, then he was directed down a wide corridor, through a set of double doors, and then through a wide single door into Brezhnev's private study.

The houseman took his overcoat and hat, poured a cognac, then backed out of the room.

A second or two later, the door opened again and Leonid Brezhnev came in, his gait slow and somewhat unsteady, but the aura of power around him just as strong as it ever was.

Gamov was taken aback, slightly, as he was every time he came into Brezhnev's presence. But then that feeling passed, as it always did, and he waited respectfully for the man to settle himself behind his desk.

"Ilya Alexandrovich," Brezhnev said. "It is good of you to come like this on such short notice."

Gamov inclined his head but said nothing. He

sat down across from Brezhnev. This close now, he could see that the skin hung in slack folds on the older man's face and neck. And he could see in Brezhnev's eyes that he was sick. Yet . . . there still was that power!

"I've brought the Central Committee briefing with me . . ."

Brezhnev waved him off. "I am certain you will comport yourself well in the briefing. Make certain Andropov gets a copy beforehand."

Gamov had picked up his briefcase, he set it back beside his chair, his eyes narrowed. If need be, he thought, he could have Reza return to his dacha, and fetch some of the files. It would take less than an hour. If there was a power play now, he would be ready for it.

"I need your help."

Gamov nodded. "Of course."

"I have appointed a special state committee to investigate the recent assassination attempt against me," Brezhnev said.

Gamov was even more confused. He supposed the KGB's first directorate, would be handling that . . . and handling it well, now that Andropov had stepped down as the Komitet's chairman.

"The committee is composed of men at all levels of government whom I can trust. I want you to head the group."

Gamov almost laughed out loud. But he kept his composure. "I would be delighted to serve, Comrade First Secretary."

"Find out who tried to kill me, Ilya Alexandrovich. Find them and punish them. This is a cancer on our society that must be ruthlessly excised."

"I thought the assassins had all died in the attempt."

Brezhnev nodded. "They did. But there were others. Planners. Organizers. Certain notes and pamphlets were found in their vehicle."

I will find them, comrade," Gamov said softly. "Rest assured I will make things right for our people."

The border gates had been opened and the train had been stopped just within the Soviet Union near Vyborg. All the passengers were required to get off, and walk down to the customs and immigration hut about a hundred yards away. It was snowing very hard now; the wind whipped around the train and howled through the woods on either side of the tracks.

Briggs trudged with the group from his car up to the hut, where they were let in three at a time. Inside, the shack was very warm, and the three cross-looking immigration officials were sweating profusely. Yet their ties were tight, and their uniform collars were buttoned as high as they would go. It was the typical Soviet mentality.

Briggs had heard a lot of shouting from inside, and from the opposite door most of the people coming out of the hut seemed shaken, some of them terrified.

The door opened, and Briggs was admitted along with two others. He had his external and internal passports ready along with his identification, work card and party card.

He strode up to one of the desks, and slapped his papers down as the immigration official scowled up at him. His KGB identification book, laying open, was on top.

The official started to say something, but Briggs stared hard at him, and the man, not quite so certain now, glanced down at the neat stack of papers. His complexion whitened noticeably. He jumped up.

"Welcome home, Comrade . . ." He glanced back at the papers.

"Solkov," Briggs snapped. "Petr Nikolai Solkov. And it is hot in this sweatbox of a place, so attend to my documents and allow me to return to my seat."

"Of course, comrade," the flustered border guard said. He sat back down, and quickly shuffled through Briggs' documents, affixing the proper stamps and initials where required.

When he was finished he handed them up. "Everything is in order, comrade. I hope you had a pleasant holiday."

Briggs snapped up his papers. "I had until this moment," he said. He turned and stomped out of the hut, slamming the door behind him.

As he trudged back to his car, bent into the wind, he let out the deep breath he had been holding. He had managed his first hurdle. The tough part would begin in a day or so.

SIX

It was well after 1:00 p.m. by the time the train pulled into the station in Leningrad. They had steamed out of the snowstorm an hour earlier, but the sky to the west was very bleak. It would not be very long before the blizzard caught up with them.

Briggs took the airport bus immediately out to the field, where within half an hour he was airborne en route to Frunze Central Airfield in Moscow.

Getting into the Soviet Union had been child's play, even easier than the last time he had come in as an American embassy spook. But once he hit Moscow and began his work, the clock would begin ticking on his discovery and arrest.

It was a principle of tradecraft that had been well drummed into his head by his emigré mentors in Soho. The fact of the matter was that no matter how good you were, no matter how careful you were, no matter how many breaks came your way, you *would* be discovered sooner or later. If for no other reason than the intelligence you were producing had to be traced back sooner or later, you would be caught.

The trick then, he had been taught, was to recognize the signs and develop a feel for the closing net, and skip out just before it snapped shut on your escape.

"Think of it as a gigantic clock, attached to a stick of dynamite in your back pocket. No one can disconnect it while you're on your operation. The idea is to get the hell out just before it blows, so someone can pull the plug."

Burt Higgins had told him that, the words nearly an echo of what he had been told in London.

It was 4:00 p.m. Leningrad time, but five o'clock Moscow time when Briggs' plane landed northwest of the city. Light snow was falling from a local disturbance, but the main brunt of the big snowstorm would not hit this far east for at least another twelve hours.

Briggs hesitated for a moment at the bottom of the boarding ladder, suddenly, inexplicably disturbed. It was as if he had just walked into a spider web, the gossamer threads light against his face. He had the feeling that someone was out there in the city, waiting for him. Something knew he was here . . . knew why he was here.

The feeling only lasted a brief moment and then was gone, but it had been no less disturbing for its brevity. He stepped the rest of the way down to the tarmac, then headed into the terminal where his papers were checked and he was released.

In the terminal he had a glass of tea, bought a copy of *Izvestia* and took the bus downtown to Kropotkin, a small bar near the river across from Gorky Park, where Goetz Solchek, the Nobel Prize winning dissident, and his group regularly met, and were waiting for him to show up.

According to Higgins, Solchek knew that an American was coming to help him get out of the Soviet Union and emigrate to Israel, in return for a job. Solchek had not been told specifically what the job was to be, but he had been informed that it would be very dangerous. He had pledged his absolute cooperation.

"The man is a fanatic on the Soviet Union. He hates it and he loves it. Once he gets out, and over to Israel I think it'll be a mixed blessing for them. He's a literary giant but a real bastard. Begin would do well to negotiate directly with the Russians to keep him."

"And this is the kind of person you want me to run an operation with?" Briggs had protested.

"Solchek and his group . . . especially the group . . . are the scum of Soviet society. Most of them are murderers, rapists, thieves."

"And they're not in jail?"

"Come on, Briggs, you know better than that. The Soviet Union doesn't have the perfect police force or court system. They spend so much time chasing after imagined bogeymen, that oftentimes the real criminals slip through their hands."

"But Solchek is a real political animal. I'd think

92

they'd be watching him all the time."

Higgins had to smile. "That's the beauty of it, Briggs. At least that's how Phil Smythe over there explained it. Solchek holds court at a small river-front bar. Every afternoon and most of the night, until they all move off to his apartment building. While the civil cops are watching him, under direct orders from the Komitet, his people literally get away with murder."

"I'm having a hard time buying that, Burt."

Higgins shrugged. "You'll have to get over there, see what the situation is, and play it by ear."

"What I'm saying, Burt, is that you want me to set Solchek up for the fall?"

"No. Once you're in with his group, you can approach one of the others . . . unbeknownst to Solchek himself. Set him up for the fall."

"I don't like it."

"It's the best we could come up with."

Riding now into the city toward the bar where Solchek and his group hung out, Briggs recalled that conversation with Higgins in detail. And it still rankled. He wasn't going to simply barge in there, and set them up for the blame of an assassination attempt on Brezhnev. There had to be another way.

In addition, since Solchek was being watched, anyone approaching him or his group would be immediately spotted.

"Which is all right, Briggs," Higgins said, "as long as you are identified as a Russian. This has to be a Russian plot right down the line. If they got wind that we were tinkering in their internal affairs, all hell would break lose."

"This is not a good operation," Briggs had said.

"No, it's not," Higgins admitted. "But the alternative is Ilya Gamov as first party secretary."

The Bolshoi Ballet Theater was lit up, as was GUM, the department store across from the familiar onion domes of St. Basil and Red Square. He had to pay a few extra kopeks at that point to continue on, finally stepping off the nearly-full bus near the Krimskiy Bridge north of the park.

Away from the bright lights downtown, it was very dark, only a few lights from either side of the river reflecting off the ice and small amount of snow. Gorky Park had a few streetlights shining, but as Briggs walked up the street, his battered suitcase in hand, he was mostly in the shadows.

There was still a lot of early evening traffic on the bridge behind him, but the noise faded as he walked into a very rundown, seedy neighborhood. It was typical, Briggs thought, of riverfront areas anywhere in the world. It had not been so long ago, on his other assignment here in Moscow, that he had come down here. It was almost familiar to him because of that, and because of the fact it reminded him a lot of many areas in London along the Thames, or in New York along the Hudson River. The same buildings, the same bars, the same people, the same darkness.

Lights shone through the cracks in two boarded-over windows across the street, halfway down the block. It was Kropotkin's, exactly as

Higgins had described the place. He could hear loud talk and laughter from inside.

He stepped back in the darker shadows of a doorway and let his eyes adjust to the scene. In a moment or two he spotted one man in a doorway up the block from him. It was just a flash of white . . . a hand moving, at first. But then a tall, husky figure stepped out of the doorway, looked up the street, then stepped back.

Walking into the bar would be one thing, but walking in with a suitcase in hand was inviting questions.

Briggs eased his way back to the corner, then down half a block to a tumble-down shack next to a vacant lot. Making sure no one was there to see him, he ducked into the shack, and quickly opened the suitcase. He pulled out his money— several thick wads of rubles—and his American passport and the overnight bag. These last two items he buried beneath a pile of rubble near the back. His suitcase he closed and locked and hid beneath some rubble in another section of the shack. He stuffed the money in his pockets.

It would not do for long, but for at least one night he figured his things would be safe.

He ducked back outside, and made his way back around the corner, then across the street, where he entered the bar, feeling the eyes on his back, but ignoring the fact.

The noise and smoke and heat of Kropotkin's hit him like a sledge hammer between the eyes. Music was playing from a very old tape recorder in a corner at one end of the long marble bar. At the opposite end of the bar a very drunk, old man was reciting poetry, his eyes glazed over as he stared out into space at nothing. Over that were the raised voices of at least fifty or sixty men, and as many women—all of them dressed shabbily, and nearly all of them very drunk.

An old woman in a filthy dress, a babushka on her head, staggered up to Briggs and threw her arm around his shoulder. "Aren't we the fancy one," she slurred. Her language was Russian but her accent and inflection would have been instantly understood by a woman from Soho, or a girl from Greenwich Village.

Briggs kissed her on the cheek. "I came to see Solchek. Is he here?"

"Depends," she said, stepping back and appraising him.

Briggs had to smile. "If I was from the police or from the Komitet, I would already know what he looked like, and wouldn't have to ask the likes of you, now, wouldn't I."

She cackled, stepped aside and pointed toward the corner away from the bar. The crowd parted, and Briggs was staring across the room into the eyes of one of the largest men he had ever seen. It was Solchek. There was no mistaking his huge, bear-like appearance. His hair was long and shaggy, his nose was very large and hooked, and his eyes huge, dark and luminous. Briggs could almost feel the heat and the vibrations coming off the man.

"*Spahsheba bahlshaya,*" Briggs said to the old woman, and he moved over to the bar. "What does Comrade Solchek customarily drink?'' he asked the large woman behind the bar.

"Cognac.''

"Give me a bottle of your best and two glasses.''

When the cognac came, he paid for it, and took the bottle across the room. Solchek had been watching him all the while. Although the noise in the bar had not ceased the room had quieted down considerably. The patrons either already knew who he was and were curious as to what would happen next; or they felt, as Briggs was beginning to feel, that a confrontation was brewing.

The big dissident sat with his back against the wall, behind a large round table. Eight or ten others sat with him, most of them men, but two of them women. The tension around the table was almost electric, and Briggs found his gaze straying from Solchek to the others . . . in particular to the young woman at the writer's left. Briggs figured her at perhaps twenty-five or twenty-six. She was very good looking, in a dark, Siberian—almost oriental—way, and she was staring at him, her lips pursed, her dark, liquid eyes wide.

There was an empty chair which Briggs hooked with his right foot and pulled out. He poured Solchek a glass of the liquor and passed it across. Then he poured himself a drink and held his glass up. Solchek raised his in salute and they both drank.

Briggs poured them both another, then sat down. Solchek leaned forward.

"You had no trouble finding us?'' the big man

asked. His voice was low, almost as if he was growling.

"None," Briggs replied. "Although I don't know if it was such a good idea . . . meeting here like this. We are being watched."

Solchek laughed out loud. "What? You mean by poor Andrevich out there?" He laughed again. "From time to time we send him out a drink. Sometimes something to eat. A little snack, you know. He really appreciates it."

The others around the table laughed as well, except for Briggs and the sloe-eyed girl.

"And when you leave here. Does he follow you home?"

Solchek shrugged. "Yes and no. Sometimes when his shift is done, he allows us to make our way to my apartment alone. But his relief man always shows up a minute or two later."

"How about the back of your building?"

"There is one there as well. But they are watching me. Photographing for when the time comes for my trial. So, except for that they are harmless. We can come and go as we please . . . that is all of you can. I always have my little weasel friends."

"Then we should send rat poison out with the next drink to Andrevich," sloe-eyed said. Her voice was very soft. Gentle.

Solchek laughed so hard he had to hold his stomach. "I have a better idea," he sputtered. "Instead of rat poison we'll send him out some love potion, so that he will become a frustrated old man watching a woman he cannot have, yet desiring her beyond all reason."

Sloe-eyed smiled seductively. "Who might the woman be?"

"You," Solchek said menacingly, and he stared pointedly at Briggs.

Briggs smiled, and raised his glass. "No love potion here, just cognac and a job to do."

"Just so," Solchek said. "We will remain here until it is our customary time to leave. If we go too early, even a dullard such as Andrevich might get suspicious."

"I'll need a place to stay. At least for a day or two."

"There are rooms in my building."

Briggs nodded, and he happened to notice out of the corner of his eye that two men were seated at the end of the bar, going through the suitcase he had just hidden in the shack. His overnight bag was laying on the bar beside it.

"Excuse me," he said. He got up and went over to them. "Pardon me, comrades, but you have my things there."

Both men looked up at Briggs, but they ignored him as they turned back to looking through his things.

Briggs tapped one of them on the shoulder, and when the man turned around, Briggs stepped back and clipped him neatly on the jaw. He fell sideways, his stool tipping around the corner of the bar, sending him sprawling.

The second man jumped back, a knife suddenly in his hand as he dropped into the classic fighter's crouch.

Briggs held both hands out, palms up. "You don't want to do this, my friend," he said moving toward the man.

"Who the hell do you think you are, coming in here like this?" the man said, shifting the knife from his right hand to his left and back. He was definitely a street fighter.

Briggs figured he had only two choices now. He could either face the man and fight it out, possibly getting nicked in the action, and almost certainly being forced to kill him. Or he could defuse the situation the easy way.

The bar had gotten fairly quiet, and many of the patrons had formed a semi-circle around Briggs and the other man. It was obvious they wanted to see a fight.

"Come one," the man with the knife kept saying. "Come on."

"Oh, hell," Briggs said, and he turned his back on the man as if he was going to simply walk away. At that moment, however, he placed all his weight on his left foot, the loose feeling coming over his entire body. He felt more than heard the man rushing up behind him. At the last moment, he spun around, bunching up the muscles in his right arm as he swung. His fist connected solidly with the man's chin, sending him off his feet, crashing against a table, his eyes fluttering, and blood spurting from his broken nose.

The pain drove all the way up into Briggs' shoulder, and he winced as he held his bloodied fist. "Bloody hell," he said to himself.

He went to the bar, and repacked his things,

including his overnight bag which contained his American passport, into the suitcase. He passed it over to the bartender.

"I don't want to be seen carrying this around. Could someone get it up to Solchek's apartment without trouble?"

"Of course," the woman said. But she refused any money when Briggs tried to pay.

He went back to the table and sat down. Solchek poured him another cognac.

"Come," the big man said, "it's time to relax now. There will be plenty of hours later tonight and tomorrow for us to talk about how we shall get my large, ugly frame out of Mother Russia, and across to the Promised Land."

It was late—sometime between two and three in the morning—before a very drunk Solchek got to his feet and announced it was time to move along.

En masse, at least twenty people from the bar surrounded Solchek. At the big man's bidding, Briggs and they left the bar, singing and stumbling up the street.

There were so many people around him that Briggs could not see if they were being followed, but he assumed they were. From time to time, however, as they walked, he did catch a glimpse of the sloe-eyed girl who had remained by Solchek's side all evening. Each time he caught sight of her, she was staring at him with her wonderful eyes. Little alarms were tugging at Briggs' nerve endings; the girl was trouble, very large trouble.

Yet she was so damned intriguing.

They crossed the street a half dozen blocks from Kropotkin's, went through an iron gate, then down a steeply sloping gravel driveway to a series of buildings directly on the river.

Just before they entered the center, five-story building, Briggs looked back over his shoulder up at the road. A man wearing a long dark overcoat and a fur hat was looking down at them. As Briggs watched, the man raised something to his face. It was a camera, Briggs supposed, with ultra-sensitive film.

Then they were in the building, trudging up the stairs all the way to the fifth floor where they all crowded into Solchek's large, book-lined, surprisingly pleasant apartment.

Several of the women, including the sloe-eyed girl, brought out vodka and cognac and glasses, bread and cheese and even a small sausage. Someone else put on some American rock and roll and a few of the couples began to dance.

Solchek pulled Briggs aside after a bit, and, with a mouthful of bread and cheese, asked what job he would be asked to do in return for his escape from Russia. The man was drunk, and greasy sweat seemed to roll off his thick face, into the dirty folds of his massive neck. He reeked of onions and cabbage and booze and something else that Briggs didn't want to think too hard or long about.

"In the morning," Briggs said. "There will be time to talk in the morning."

"I talk now. It is best late at night. My creative

juices flow best."

"Mine don't," Briggs said. "Now, where can I sleep for the night? It has been a very long day for me."

Solchek's eyes narrowed.

"You want out of Russia, and I need some work done. It will be a fair exchange. But on my terms, comrade, on my terms."

"I could break you in two with my bare hands, tough man."

"Then you'd stay here and rot."

Solchek's nostrils flared. They had kept their voices down, but several of his friends in the group were watching. None of them looked friendly.

Slowly, the harsh expression on the big man's face softened and he grinned. "If you need your beauty rest, then we will talk in the morning. I am a fair man. And I want to help you."

"And I will help you in return," Briggs said.

Solchek waved for one of the women. "Marsa," he called out.

A short, stocky woman, in her mid to late forties came over. Solchek greeted her with a hug. "Our guest here . . ." He looked at Briggs in amazement. "Your name is Solkov. But I don't know the rest."

"Petr Nikolai," Briggs said.

Solchek beamed. "Petr Nikolai here is tired. Show him where he can sleep. His suitcase will be there."

"In the morning," Briggs said.

Solchek nodded, and Briggs followed Marsa out

of the apartment, and down to the fourth floor, where she showed him a tiny, efficiency apartment.

"Where are the people?" Briggs asked turning on the one small light in the tiny room.

Marsa shrugged. "The gulags. Who knows?"

Briggs looked around.

"The couch folds out as a bed. And there may be something to eat in the cupboard, if you're hungry. Otherwise come upstairs with us. You will not starve."

"Thanks," Briggs said.

The woman went back out in the corridor, but before she left, she looked back in at Briggs and shook her head. "You are trouble. I can feel it."

SEVEN

The wind steadily rose in the night from the north-west, so that by the gray dawn it shrieked around the corners of the building, rattled the windows and sent cold drafts scurrying everywhere.

Briggs had taken a bath down at the end of the corridor, and had crawled into the warm bed immediately afterwards. He was only vaguely aware, through the early morning hours, of the rising wind, but something woke him up shortly after dawn, and he opened his eyes.

The sloe-eyed girl stood beside his bed, peeling off her sweater. She was wearing nothing beneath it, her large, firm breasts dark, her nipples already erect.

She tossed the sweater aside, and started to peel off her slacks when she realized that he was awake and was watching her. She smiled, her teeth very white against her olive skin. "Petr Nikolai," she said softly. "I like your name."

"This will bring trouble. . . ."

"Esfir," she said. "And it will not bring trouble for me." She laughed, and finished taking off her slacks then her panties. The small tuft of public hair was jet black.

Briggs held the covers back and she crawled into bed. She was cold, and for a time Briggs just held her close, but then as she began to warm up, she began kissing his neck, then his chest and his belly, working her way down, until she had him in her mouth.

He looked down at her and he froze. Her entire back, her tiny buttocks and even the backs of her long, lovely legs were crisscrossed with scars and with long, red marks, some of which were obviously recent.

She looked up, realizing that he was no longer with her, and then an instant later realizing why. She sat up. "Does it bother you?" she asked.

"What happened to you, Esfir?"

"It does not matter. Only here and now is of consequence."

"Was it Solchek?"

She came into his arms, but held a finger across his lips "Please," she purred.

He pulled her finger away and held her close for a long time. She began to shiver.

"He is a very large and powerful man," Briggs said, a rage bubbling just beneath his control.

She pulled back and looked into his eyes. "He is a very strange, violent man, Petr. Be very careful of him. He does not like you, nor does he trust you. But you have something he wants . . . at least for the moment. But watch for when he tires of playing with you."

"But why do you let him do this to you?" Briggs asked.

"Hush now," she said pushing him back on the bed, and soon they were making slow, very gentle love. She cried out once as he entered her, but then her passion mounted, and their lovemaking became more urgent. Only later did Briggs realize that it had been the first time for her. She had been a virgin.

Esfir left around nine, but it wasn't until noon that Marsa came down to say that Solchek was awake and ready to talk. Briggs had been watching the snowstorm and the frozen river, trying to think out his next steps when she came. He followed her back up.

Solchek was sitting nude on a pile of cushions in the middle of the floor. His body was grossly bloated, and almost completely covered with hair. Briggs' first impression was that he was looking at a huge ape in a zoo. But then Solchek looked up and smiled.

"You had a good sleep?"

Briggs nodded. There were several others in the room (all of them clothed). They were eating dark bread and what appeared to be borscht.

"Come in . . . come in, sit down and have something to eat with us."

Marsa brought him a bowl and a glass of tea.

She ladled some borscht for him, and pulled off a large piece of bread. Then he sat down cross-legged beside Solchek. Esfir was not here, but just thinking about her back and legs made Briggs' gut churn. It would be so easy, he told himself.

"So, Petr Nikolai, or whatever your name is, let us get down to business. We can be of help to each other."

"I'll get you out of the Soviet Union," Briggs said. In a pine box, if he had his way about it.

"In exchange for what services?"

"There is a man very high in the government whom I must know about."

"What do you wish to know about this man. I know many men in high positions in the government," Solchek said laughing.

"I need to know everything about this man. Where he lives. Where he works, and what he does there. I need to know what he eats, about his lovers or his family. I want to know everything there is to know about him. The sooner that happens, the sooner you can get out."

Solchek nodded. "A tall order, but certainly not impossible for my people, under my direction. Who is this mystery man you have such a burning desire to find out everything about, the old whore-master Brezhnev himself?"

"Very close," Briggs said. "Ilya Alexandrovich Gamov."

Solchek belched in surprise. The others around the room stiffened.

"Brezhnev might be easier," Solchek said in amazement.

Briggs held his silence.

Solchek looked at his people, then back at Briggs. "Gamov is a special aide to Brezhnev. He reports to the Central Committee and the Politburo. He's also nominal head of the KGB's Second Chief Directorate. He and Yuri Andropov are both in line to take over when the old man dies." Solchek's eyes narrowed. "Is that what this is all about? You are meddling in our politics?"

"I want nothing more from your people than information about Gamov. I want to know where he goes, how he gets there, and what he does."

"That will take time."

"We do not have much time," Briggs said. "As a matter of fact I don't think you have much time left. So if you want to get out, you'd better help, and help quickly."

Solchek appeared to think about it for a moment or two. Then he nodded. "And while all this is going on, where will you be?"

"That is none of your business."

Solchek flared, but Briggs held him off.

"If any of your people follow me, I'll disappear and our deal will be off. Is that clear?"

Solchek smiled after a bit. "Perfectly," he said. "We will begin at once with what we already know. It shall be the base from which we shall spread our wings and fly."

Marsa was gazing at Solchek as if he were a god. Briggs wondered what kind of a hold he had on these people. Christ. It reminded him of Charles Manson and his cult.

"Gamov has a very large dacha outside the city,

to the northeast. Very lovely from what I've been told. Very old."

"I will need a map," Briggs said. "One with enough detail so I can pinpoint the place."

"There are such maps, although it might be easier and certainly much safer to simply draw you a sketch."

"As long as it's reasonably accurate," Briggs said.

"I know nothing of his work habits, although I would assume he has an office at Lubyanka."

"How about Gorky Missile Base? What do you know if it?"

This time Solchek sucked his breath. "You *are* after very large game, Petr Nikolai."

"Gamov, I am told, goes there quite often. It is evidently very important to him."

Solchek shook his head. "We know nothing about the place."

"Not even its location?"

"West of the city. Perhaps fifty miles."

"You could pinpoint it on a sketch map as well?"

"Are you a saboteur as well as an assassin?"

"I'm neither," Briggs said.

"What then?"

"A gatherer of information. Nothing more."

Marsa's eyes were narrowed. She looked from Briggs back to Solchek. "He is a man with a vendetta. I can see it in his eyes."

Solchek managed a slight smile. "So am I," he said. He snapped his fingers at one of the others in the room, and the young man scurried to the bookcases, where he fetched a large writing board, paper and pen.

Briggs came to Solchek's side as the man began sketching out Moscow and its environs, beginning with the Moscow River which curved like a snake in agony through the city. At the center was Red Square. To the south Moscow State University. To the east, the military academy. To the west, Frunze Central Airfield. And to the north Dzerzhinsky Park and the Palace Museum.

He sketched in a few of the main highways, then located Gamov's dacha in the birch forests.

"Any side roads through that area?" Briggs asked.

Solchek thought a moment, and sketched two that ran from the main highways back into the forest.

"There may be others that I know nothing about," Solchek said.

Briggs studied the map over Solchek's shoulder for a minute or two. "How about Gorky?"

"This is Leningradskoye Road, past the airport. The missile base is, as I have said, about fifty miles to the west."

"How would I know it?"

"You are going there?"

"Either me, or your people. We will need a car. Gamov must be followed."

"I can get a car. But it will be very expensive." He pointed to the increasing snowstorm out the window. "And until this is over with, you would not get far. Certainly not out to Gorky."

Briggs nodded. But the snowstorm was just the

111

cover he wanted. "When can I have the car?"

Solchek glared at him for a moment or two. "It would be too dangerous to bring it here. I will give you the address of a garage where you can pick it up right now if you want . . . and if you have the money."

"Very good," Briggs said. He folded the sketch map and put it in his pocket. Then he pulled out one of the packets of rubles. It was far too much money for the use of the car, but it would keep Solchek and the others quiet for a while. He dropped it on the writing board. "Use this as you see fit. If there are other expenses . . ."

Solchek made no move to touch the money. The others were staring at it.

"There'll be more if your people work fast," Briggs said.

"This is not for money," Solchek said.

"I know. But the money will help."

Solchek wrote down the address of the garage, which he said was within walking distance of the apartment. He assured Briggs that the registration was up to date, legal and could not be traced back to anyone in the group.

"I will be at Kropotkin's tonight," Briggs said before he left. "I'll expect at least some preliminary information."

Back up in his room, Briggs pulled on his boots and overcoat, donned a fur hat and gloves, and tromped down the stairs to the ground floor.

The corridor was very cold. He could see his own breath. But outside, the cold was stunning, well below zero.

Esfir, bundled up in fur-lined boots and a parka, was waiting for him outside. The cold didn't really seem to bother her.

"I am coming with you," she shouted over the wind.

"It's too dangerous," Briggs shouted.

"I don't care about him. I am coming with you."

"I mean from the police," Briggs said. They held their heads close together so they could hear.

"The police don't care about us. All they have eyes for is Solchek. Everyone in the West knows him, so whenever he does something it hits the newspapers. The police don't want him to get out of hand. But we can come and go as we please."

"I don't want you with me. Go back inside. Keep an eye on Solchek," Briggs said, and he broke away from her, trudged up the hill to the snow-covered street, then turned east, away from the river.

Solchek's civil police shadow was in a parked car just up the street from the apartment building, and he paid absolutely no attention to Briggs as he passed. Yet the feeling that someone knew he was in Moscow, and knew why he was here, continued to grow.

Briggs had very little trouble finding the small garage in a dingy neighborhood just off Ordynka B Street, although it took him nearly an hour to get to it in the wind and snow.

A man opened the door from the apartment

113

above and came down, his coat open and flapping. They shook hands.

"Inside, inside," the man said, pulling open the garage door.

Briggs helped him, and they slipped inside. A very small, incredibly beat-up car that looked very much like the smallest model Fiat was backed into the garage. The man patted its roof top with affection. "This is a wonderful machine. You will treat it well."

"Will it run?" Briggs asked.

"Of course," the man said, hurt. "There is a full tank of gas, and another fifteen liters in the boot."

"I mean will the engine start and keep running in this cold?"

"Yes, yes, certainly. This is a Moscow car. A Muskova. Very good. Well built. You will see."

The door creaked open the rest of the way, and Esfir came in.

"Ah, your friend," the man said. "She was waiting for you. She explained everything." He handed Briggs the key, then nodded effusively and left the garage.

"What the hell are you doing here?" Briggs asked.

"You would never have gotten the car without me," she said. She turned and pushed the garage door all the way open. "As soon as you're out, I'll close it," she said.

Briggs got behind the wheel, and the car started up surprisingly easy, despite the cold. He had to clash the gears to get them to engage, and he eased out of the garage, into the storm, then stopped, as Esfir closed and latched the door. He could have easily continued down the street, leaving her behind. But something held him back.

She climbed in the passenger seat. "I know a shortcut," she said.

Briggs flipped on the defroster and windshield wipers, and they headed out to Ordynka, then across the river, bypassing Red Square past GUM, and finally onto Yaroslavskoye Road which was reasonably well-plowed, so that he could speed up slightly.

They had not talked since they had left the garage. She was the first to break the silence.

"The snow is very beautiful," she said.

"But cold."

"No," she disagreed. "In my city of Yakutsk winter is much harsher than here. Very much."

"Siberia?"

"The Republic of Yakut, actually," she said. "But it was very cold."

"How did you come here, to Moscow?" Briggs asked. There was something indefinably sad about the woman. Besides the beatings she had received at the hands of Solchek . . . or perhaps hand-in-hand with them.

"My parents sold me to him . . . when I was fifteen," she said. "There was no money. My parents, my grandmother and my brothers, would have starved."

"How did they . . . come to Solchek? Why him?"

"He came to them," she said. "He was a very

important writer then. It was twelve years ago. He had not won the Nobel Prize yet, so the authorities were not after him. He had his writer's union card, and was very highly praised. He came to our town to speak at the college. I don't know how he found us, though there were hundreds of parents then who would have sold their daughters. But he came, the deal was made, and the next day I came back to Moscow with him."

The road seemed to run through an endless string of neighborhoods, each with its own little shopping area, parks, and independent farmer's market areas. There was very little traffic out and about, although two jeeps and five military trucks had passed them on the way out of the city minutes earlier.

"It must have been very frightening for you," Briggs said.

"It was," she said in a very small voice. "As soon as we reached Moscow, the very first night, I found out what kind of a man he was." She looked earnestly at Briggs. "Petr Nikolai, do you know he never had sex with me? Not once in those twelve years? Not ordinary sex. He made me do things with my hands and my mouth, but never my . . . body. And then he beat me."

"Why didn't you run away?" Briggs could feel his anger mounting again.

"I did," she cried. "Many times. But each time the police brought me back, and the beatings became worse for a time. Finally they told me that if I ran away again, they would throw me in a gulag, and I would become the plaything for the gangs.'' She hung her head, tears in her eyes. "I did not try to run away after that.''

"Does he know . . . about last night?''

She looked up, and shook her head. "He ordered me to come along with you. To take you to bed. He wants me to watch you, and tell him everything you say and do.''

Briggs was seething with conflicting emotions as they finally cleared the last of the city, past the All-Union Agricultural Exhibition, and he had to slow way down in order to keep the car under control and on the road. One part of him wanted to turn around, go back to the apartment building, and kill Solchek with his bare hands. The man was depraved. Another part of him wanted to keep going with Esfir, back across the Finnish border. Howard, or if need be, Sir Roger, could find a place for her. At least she'd be safe.

Yet he knew that he could do neither . . . at least not yet.

An hour later, he recognized one of the turnoffs that circled behind Gamov's dacha, and he pulled over to the side of the highway, and put the tire chains he found in the trunk on the back wheels. The going would be a hell of a lot tougher back here than it was on the main road.

The images flickering on the screen were of two women—one of them young and very beautiful, the other older, shorter, and very stocky. They were both nude, and the younger woman was chasing the older around the bedroom. It was a

117

disgusting scene, made all the more revolting by the pendulous breasts of the older woman, the cesarian scar on her abdomen, and the crisscross of blue veins at the backs of her chubby legs.

She was Larissa Romanov, a beautiful name for such an ugly creature, Gamov thought. *Colonel* Romanov, special aidé-de-camp for Andropov's number two man.

Reza had set up the projector in the bedroom, and then had laid in a fire on the grate. It was very pleasant in the room now, and lying there nude on the silk sheets Gamov felt a thrill of anticipation, as he watched the images on the screen, and listened for Reza to finish in the shower.

All last night and all day today, he had gone through a particularly tense time. On the one hand he was going through the motions with the silly committee, trying to find who was responsible for the assassination attempt on Brezhnev.

Yet on the other hand, he was beginning to feel like a claustrophobic man in a small, dark room, where the walls were beginning to close in on him.

Someone was out there, coming for him. He could feel it thick in the air especially in Moscow today, but now even out here.

Guilt, perhaps, he told himself. Or perhaps his feelings were justified. It was possible that Brezhnev had gotten wind of these films, and had sent his spies out to learn more.

It was even more likely that the bastard, Andropov had sent his agents to snoop around.

Well, it was nearly too late for any of that. Soon, Gamov thought, very soon the jaws of his little steel trap would close, and he would be the undisputed master.

The shower had stopped, and the adjoining bathroom door opened. Reza stood there nude, and Gamov could feel himself responding.

"Come over here, you naughty boy," he said smiling, forgetting all his concerns for the moment.

EIGHT

It was late afternoon and getting dark already when Briggs finally stopped the car next to a utility pole on a narrow track that had branched off from the back road Solchek had sketched. He left the car running, and the windshield wipers flapping, but he doused the lights. No one would be coming along this road this afternoon, certainly not in these conditions.

"What is it?" Esfir asked. She looked outside into the swirling snow.

Briggs looked up at the utility pole. The electric wires ran overhead across the road, then disappeared into the storm. But they ran in the direction of Gamov's dacha. According to Solchek, there wasn't anything else out here, so the electric lines probably did serve Gamov's estate. And under these conditions Briggs did not think he'd have much problem getting close to the house without detection. The problem came when he asked himself why he had come out here? Why was he taking this risk? His only answer was insurance. But now that he was here, this close, the feeling that someone was waiting for him had grown even stronger.

"I want you to stay here, in the car," Briggs said, turning to her.

Her eyes widened, and she reached out for him. "What's wrong? Where are you going?"

"If someone comes, tell them you could not drive farther in this storm. Don't tell them about me."

"I'm coming with you."

"No."

"Where are you going?" she screeched. She was shaking. Briggs reached over and held her in his arms.

"It's all right," he said soothingly. "I'll just be gone for a few minutes."

"But why . . . what are you after?"

"This is where Gamov lives. I want to see his house. That's all."

"Who is this Gamov?"

Briggs explained who the man was, and what Solchek and his people were doing. It would not matter if the information that he had been here got out. In fact it would strengthen the notion that Solchek's people were working for Gamov. But it would disappoint Briggs if it did—it would mean that he was completely wrong about Esfir.

She accepted his explanation with narrowed eyes, and then she nodded. "Then you will need help."

"Yes," Briggs said. "I don't want my escape cut off. Stay here with the car."

She nodded again. "But how will I know if you are in trouble?"

"You won't," Briggs said. "Give me one hour at the outside. If I'm not back by then, go back to Solchek and tell him what happened."

"Come back to me, Petr," she said. She leaned forward and kissed him, then she sat back.

Briggs climbed out of the car, the shrieking wind and blowing snow making it nearly impossible to see a thing from up on the roadway. He quickly crossed to the other side, and plunged into the birch forest, following the overhead power lines. In the relative protection of the woods, the going was somewhat easier, the wind broken up by all the trees. It roared overhead, and at every open spot the snow had already drifted up to three or four feet. By morning this area would be impassable.

A couple of hundred yards from the road, the power lines went over a tall, wire mesh fence. There was no barbed wire at the top, nor, as far as Briggs could tell, was the fence in any way electrified or wired for alarms. That meant one of two things to Briggs. Either Gamov had never experienced any trouble out here and therefore did not expect any, or the fence was merely a property marker, and inside were patrolling guards.

Briggs hoped for the former as he climbed up over the fence, but expected the latter. Gamov was running a very dangerous operation. He would definitely have security measures around himself.

He dropped to the other side, and held there in his half crouch for a minute or so. He was edgy. He could feel the hair at the nape of his neck standing. Carefully he pulled off his right glove and reached around back beneath his coat and pulled out his stiletto. He put his glove back on, then started forward, still following the power lines.

He heard the house before he saw it, a few hundred yards up a gentle slope away from the fence. The wind through the treetops was a steady, roaring sound, but the wind whipping around the sharp edges and through the ornately carved eaves moaned like some kind of a wild animal in pain.

Cautiously he edged forward, until he managed to pick out the lit up windows.

He was at the back of the house. There were several other buildings on the property, none of which seemed to be lit up from inside, but all of which were illuminated by lights from the outside.

As he watched from the darkness in the woods, the back door opened and two men in uniforms, rifles (which even at this distance Briggs recognized as Kalashnikovs) slung over their shoulders, stepped down from the porch and marched across to one of the other buildings. They went inside, and a minute or two later, two other guards came out of the building, and went into the house. It was a changing of the guard. He had come evidently at the beginning of a new shift. Evidently, Gamov did take his security seriously.

It was one of things Briggs had hoped to learn by coming here. If Gamov was this security conscious, then he'd start to get paranoid when he realized that he was being followed by Solchek's people. Paranoid people often made mistakes. Incriminating mistakes. It would all add up in Brezhnev's mind when it came time for Gamov's trial for treason.

Smiling, Briggs turned to go back, and came face to face with two guards, their assault rifles trained on him.

"Good evening," he said pleasantly, the old loose feeling coming over him. He made no move to raise his hands. His stiletto was hidden in the folds of his thick coat.

"Put your hands on top of your head," one of the guards snapped. The other pulled out a walkie-talkie and started to raise it to his lips.

"Wait!" Briggs cried out in alarm.

The guard with the radio hesitated.

"You'll ruin everything if you report this, comrade. Believe me. My head will roll. You know how it is?"

Both guards were confused.

"Look, let me show you my identification," Briggs said, and he slowly unbuttoned his coat with his free hand.

The guard with the rifle waved his hand away, and the other one stepped forward and pulled Briggs' identification case out of his inner pocket. At that moment the man was closer to death than he had ever been, but Briggs let him back off with the ID.

They shined a flashlight on his papers which showed he was a KGB officer. Briggs nodded and smiled, as they looked up at him with new respect.

'What are you doing here . . . Captain?''

''What does it look like I am doing, idiot!''
Briggs snapped.

The guard with the radio shook his head. He
was clearly very worried. ''I'm going to have to
report this,'' he said raising the radio to his lips.

''Wait,'' Briggs said again. With these odds, at
this range, and with their heavy winter coats, his
stiletto would not be particularly effective. That
raced through his mind at the same moment he
understood what he was going to have to do.
Gamov was going to have to be put off balance.
''I have my orders,'' he said. He let the stiletto
drop.

Again the guards hesitated. But this time they
did not try to stop him as he reached inside his
coat pocket. They thought he was fishing for his
paperwork. Instead he pulled out the Graz-Buyra
automatic Higgins insisted he be armed with as a
KGB agent, and before either guard could react,
he fired two shots, the first catching the guard
with the rifle in the forehead, the second catching
the guard with the radio, who was fumbling for
his gun, in the neck.

Both guards went down in a bloody heap in the
snow, the first one dead, the second one dying.

''Christ,'' Briggs swore. He hated guns. But the
big automatic was standard Moscow Center issue.
Gamov's guards shot to death with such a weapon
would cause him a lot of worry.

The shots had been effectively muffled by the
noises of the storm, and no alarms were sounded.

125

Briggs stuffed the automatic back in its holster, picked up his stiletto and headed back to the fence as fast as he could run through the deepening snow.

It was bothersome that he had been caught off guard like that. Apparently he had stumbled across their post. But in this weather anything was possible. He just didn't want it to happen again.

He made it to the fence without trouble, and on the other side he followed his nearly filled-in tracks in the snow back up to the road.

Before he went across he re-sheathed his stiletto, looked back to make sure he had not been followed, then hurried to the car and climbed in.

The car was warm and Briggs loosened his coat. Esfir was watching him, silently, her body rigid.

"Did anyone come?" Briggs asked.

She shook her head, and they looked at each other for several long moments. He felt sorry for her. But there was no time now for him to stop and help her. She would have to hang on for a little while longer.

"Was there any trouble?" she asked.

"No," Briggs lied. He put the car in gear, flipped on the headlights, and carefully maneuvered around on the narrow, snow-clogged road until they were heading back the way they had come.

The first two steps in an impossible operation had been taken, and Briggs wasn't satisfied with either of them. It was sloppy, but if anyone was watching they would soon understand that there was some sort of a connection between Solchek's

126

people and Gamov. And after tonight, Gamov would suspect that someone from the government, perhaps his rival Andropov, perhaps Brezhnev himself, was closing in.

The entire operation was so damned tenuous. And yet there was no other way around it. If Gamov was to be ousted, he'd have to be blamed for an attempt on Brezhnev's life.

It was after eight by the time they drove back into Moscow and got the car back into the garage. Esfir brought the keys upstairs while Briggs locked up, and then together they trudged the ten blocks to Kropotkin's. The storm had slowed down to a steady, strong wind and a very hard snowfall. It was the kind of storm that would probably last at least twenty-four hours, dumping a couple of feet of snow. But the Russians were well used to this kind of weather, and their snow removal crews would be working around the clock to keep the major streets in the city open, and the major high-ways at least passable.

No one paid any attention to Briggs as he and Esfir entered the club and made their way back to where Solchek was holding court with a dozen of his cronies. Some of them he recognized from the apartment. But one of them, dressed in a baggy, gray suit and old overcoat, was a cop—Briggs was almost one hundred percent sure of it.

Esfir went dutifully around the table and sat down beside Solchek, who looked up at Briggs and beamed. But there was something in his eyes

. . . a warning?

"You must have had a wonderful supper with my Esfir," Solchek said.

"Actually we didn't have anything to eat. I'm famished," Briggs said, taking a chair across the table from the baggy-suited man. He looked pointedly at him. "In fact we were feeding the pigeons."

"In this weather?" the man asked.

Briggs smiled. "It was very difficult, you know. But we can't just let them die. The poor little dears."

A funny look came over the man's face.

"I mean . . . honestly," Briggs said, slurring his words. He reached out for the man's hand.

"What the hell . . ." the baggy-suited man said, jumping up.

"Do not be afraid, Andrevich," Solchek boomed.

The cop looked from Solchek to Briggs and back again, as he sidestepped out from behind the table. There was a disgusted look on his face, as he glanced at Briggs again, then he spit on the floor, turned and stomped out of the building. Everyone laughed, except for Solchek who watched Briggs through narrowed eyes.

As the laughter died, someone brought Briggs and Esfir a plate of bread, sausage, cheese, smoked salmon and borscht. Briggs poured himself a stiff shot of cognac and began to eat.

"You were busy this afternoon?" Solchek said. "I don't think you went all the way out to Gorky."

Briggs looked up startled. Solchek laughed.

"They are to be trusted. All of them here. Without me they would be dead, and they all know it," the big dissident said. He laughed again, the sound humorless.

"You have some information for me?" Briggs asked.

"Only in the negative sense," Solchek said after a slight hesitation.

Briggs waited for him to continue.

"No one knows very much about Gamov. He's a very secretive man, from what we can gather. It goes beyond even what you would expect of someone so high in government, someone connected with the Komitet. On Andropov we can find things, but on Gamov . . ."

"Did any of your people manage to make visual contact with him today?"

"No. I suspect he's at his dacha during this storm. His apartment was dark."

"And where did this information come from?"

"Friends," Solchek said defensively.

Good, Briggs thought. Already the word was going out: Someone is interested in Gamov. Who? Why?

"There is a way, however, to get all the information we want. Just a possibility."

"What's that?"

"He has a personal secretary. Reza Makat. A Muslim. A very old family. There are certain relatives still around, from what I have been told, who don't approve of this Reza, but who still have contact with him."

"I'm after information on Gamov, not his secretary," Briggs snapped.

Solchek leaned forward and slammed his fist on the table, his face suddenly red. "I'll get your information on Gamov, but Reza Makat is mine. Before I leave I'm going to play with him, like his kind have played with me."

"What do you have in mind, killing him?" Briggs asked, very careful to keep his voice in absolute control. No sudden moves now.

"I have a much better idea than that," the big man said. "He has a sister. I wonder how he would feel if his sister was raped and then killed?"

"You would have that done?" Briggs asked. The bar was deathly still.

Solchek leaned even closer. "No, I wouldn't have it done . . . I would do it with the greatest of pleasures. That and more." He smiled. "That and much more. Let them suffer as I have suffered."

Any doubts that Briggs had about Rudyard Howard's selection of Solchek for the fall in this operation—any last twinges of conscience he had about ruthlessly setting an innocent man up—left him. Between Esfir's story and the marks on her body, and Solchek's own statements now, Briggs was getting a very good picture of the man. It was a wonder the Russians hadn't kicked him out of the country years ago, instead of keeping him here.

Briggs got up, taking his cognac with him. He went over to the end of the bar, and leaned up against the tin top. A moment later the two men nearest pushed away and moved to the other end of the bar.

In the mirror behind the bar, Briggs watched Solchek ponderously make his way from behind the table and move up to the bar.

They drank, elbow to elbow, for a few moments in silence. Solchek smelled of a combination of cloves and cognac.

"I have bigger game in mind than this secretary of Gamov," Briggs said.

"Other than Gamov? Or the man himself?"

"Someone else."

"Bigger game. Andropov or Brezhnev himself?" Solchek said. Briggs could hear in the man's voice that he was interested.

"Brezhnev."

"The old man. What would you have us do? Kill him?" Solchek shook his head. "He will die soon enough."

"It's more sophisticated than that, believe me. You want to strike back for all the suffering—this is your chance."

Solchek looked at him for a while. "You are an intriguing man, Petr Nikolai. You have us follow Gamov, then tell me of a dark plot against the old whoremaster in Red Square."

For just a moment, Briggs hesitated. But then he said, the hell with it. Solchek was probably the one man in all of the Soviet Union whom he could trust implicitly with his plan. Solchek was the one man who would never go to the authorities. There was too much at stake for him.

"What would happen if someone tried to assassinate Brezhnev, but failed, and the plot

131

could concretely be blamed on Gamov?"

Solchek's eyes went wide, and his nostrils flared. He started to laugh, but then held himself in check. He was excited. "You *are* a devious man, Petr." He chuckled. "I don't even care to ask what is in this for you, because it simply does not matter. This is delicious. The repercussions will last for years."

Briggs nodded. "But we need more information on Gamov in order to come up with a sure scheme to blame it on him. His time schedule, for one. His habits, as far as we can possibly know them. His friends. Anything."

"Indeed," Solchek said. "And fast before the old man dies of natural causes." The big dissident laughed again, barely able to control himself. "That would be a shame."

The snow storm had not let up through the night. Esfir had come down to Briggs' apartment around two and they had made love. It was nearly noon now, and Briggs stood off to one side in the ladies' dress department in GUM, while Esfir was trying on a dress in one of the fitting rooms.

After he had left Kropotkin's last night, he had left instructions for a meet at the letter drop Higgins had said would be set up for him at the Kamenyy Bridge, across the river from the Kremlin.

He knew that Esfir would probably be with him, so he had set this place up.

He spotted Phil Smythe from the British

Embassy the moment the man walked in. His wife was with him.

Esfir came out, excited about the dress, but Briggs made her take two others in to try on. Smythe did the same with his wife, then came over to where Briggs was standing.

"How is everything going?"

"Very good," Briggs said, not looking at the man. "Anything new for me?"

"Nothing."

"Listen. I need the papers, and uniform of a Polish officer. An engineer, here on temporary duty."

"For where?"

"Gorky Missile Base." Briggs could hear Smythe sucking his breath.

"A tall order. I don't know."

"I need it as soon as possible. Tomorrow. The day after, at the latest."

"You'll need a gate pass, and some kind of transportation. You'll also need a background here in Moscow, probably. How many entries?"

"At least two, possibly more."

"Are you trying to become a fixture?"

"No, just familiar." Briggs chanced a look at Smythe. The man was worried.

"I won't even ask you what this is all about."

"Can you do it for me?" Briggs asked.

"I'll give it a whack, old top. Best I can offer."

"We'll have to set up a meet for the transfer somewhere. I'll keep watch on our letter drop and the alternate for your instructions."

"If this bloody snow ever stops . . ." Smythe

133

said, but Esfir came back out and Briggs went to her. When they were finished, he looked for Smythe but the man was already gone.

NINE

Briggs spent most of the next day in his apartment below Solchek's. Late in the afternoon Esfir came to him, and they made slow, gentle love. There was a lot of pent-up passion inside of her, but it seemed as if she was afraid of letting it out for fear she'd not be able to go back upstairs.

The snow had slowed down and the wind had all but died finally, so that many of the streets in Moscow were cleared. Briggs was becoming anxious to get his plan in motion.

Around six, Solchek sent one of his people down to Briggs to tell him that Gamov had been spotted leaving Lubyanka and heading over to the Kremlin. He had remained within the walls for a half hour, then headed out Yaroslavskoye Road—presumably back to his dacha.

There would be much more information this evening at Kropotkin's, the man promised.

Briggs sent Esfir back upstairs just before seven, about the time Solchek and the others began gathering to go to the bar, promising that as soon as he bathed, he would be along.

She looked at him funny. "You bathe too much," she said. "It is unusual."

Briggs had to smile. Higgins had told him about the Russians' dislike for bathing during the winter. He said he had gone to the Bolshoi in Moscow one midwinter evening, when he had been assigned embassy duty here. The stench from dirty bodies was so intense that the next day the entire Western diplomatic corps complained. Later, he had been told, deoderant that could be sprayed directly on the clothes became available at the door. It had been called Stalin's Breath, and smelled worse than unwashed bodies.

"I'm an unusual fellow," Briggs replied, lightly. But she didn't completely buy the explanation. He told himself that he would have to be careful.

It was 7:30 by the time everyone had finally left, and the building quieted down. Briggs got dressed, and went out. The civil cop who usually stood guard on the road was gone. He had evidently followed Solchek.

On the road, Briggs turned left, instead of right toward the club, and hurried up the street toward the Kámenyy Bridge. It was dark, and although the wind and snow had died, the temperature had plunged to below zero . . . and this for early October. This was going to be a very hard winter.

Out of long habit, Briggs did not make a

straight line for his letter drop at the bridge, instead he ducked down back alleys, doubled back, studied shop windows, gazed up at street signs as if he was a man out for a walk and not a hundred percent sure of where he was, or where he was going.

The closer he got to the bridge, the more foot traffic he encountered. Half of Moscow, it seemed, was out for an evening stroll, despite the frigid weather, or out on business after the first major snowstorm of the winter had kept them cooped up for a day and half.

Three blocks from the bridge he realized that he was being followed by one of Solchek's people. It was an older man, wearing a dark, tattered coat, and a moth-eaten fur cap.

In the next block, Briggs ducked down into the subway, and then into the restroom. He waited there for a few minutes, then cautiously went back out on the wide, very clean platform, lit by lovely chandeliers. There were a lot of people, but there was no sign of Solchek's man, who evidently figured that Briggs had jumped on a train.

Outside again, there still was no sign of the man, yet Briggs approached the bridge with extreme caution. It would not do at this point to have this contact uncovered. Not by Solchek, not by anyone.

When Briggs was certain he was in the clear, he doubled the last two blocks back to the bridge, and headed across the river. The Pushkin Museum, Lenin Library and Red Square were all lit up, and with the fresh snow, the city looked beautiful. Nearly halfway across the bridge, Briggs slowed down, and at the fourth concrete post before the center-span light stanchion, he stopped and leaned over the wide rail, and looked down at the frozen river. There were several snow machines on the ice, and several large trucks were dumping snow from the banks.

Making sure there was no one nearby, and that no one was paying him the slightest attention, he reached down and to the left, where his fingers brushed against a single thin strand of colorless monofilament. He gathered it up and pulled it until he came to a small, flat, gray canister—similar to the metal tins that held throat lozenges. He broke the thin line with a sharp tug, and pocketed the tin.

After a bit, he straightened up, and headed back the way he had come, his step slow and deliberate, as if he were a man with absolutely nothing to hide, out for a simple afternoon stroll.

A few blocks away from the bright lights of the bridge, Briggs opened the canister, and took out the small piece of note paper it contained. In the light from a corner bakery, he was able to read the brief instruction from Smythe. It simply gave an address, and advised that someone would be there from one this morning until six. And the same on the next few nights.

He stuffed the note back in his pocket, tossed the canister down a storm sewer and crossed the street. Tonight it would be. He did not know how long he could keep Solchek and his people from doing something rash . . . or, for that matter, how long it would take for Gamov to react, and react hard.

The clock was ticking. Each hour that passed raised their risk of discovery to astronomical levels. He didn't even want to think of the risk taken by whoever was getting the MiG trainer to the lake near the Finnish border. That worry would come later when it was time to get out.

Briggs went to Kropotkin's only long enough to tell Solchek that he was going to be gone for a day or two, not to try to follow him, and to do nothing more than gather information on the elusive Gamov.

He had expected some trouble from the big dissident, and he had expected that Esfir would put up a fuss to tag along. But nothing happened. Solchek nodded, and smiled sagely, and Esfir avoided his eyes.

"If you want out of the country, you will do as I say," Briggs warned. Again Solchek nodded, and Briggs left the bar, an uneasy feeling growing at the back of his mind that Solchek was up to something.

The address on the note from Smythe was in the southeast quarter of the city past the Simonov Monastery that since Stalin had been nothing more than a museum. This area of the city was given over mostly to friendly foreigners—mostly Poles, Hungarians, Rumanians and Bulgarians. Briggs had chosen to act as a Polish officer because second only to Russian, his Polish was perfect. And at this moment, the Polish Army was getting a lot of help and aid from the Soviet Union.

The address turned out to be a third-story apartment in a very good looking ten-story apartment building. Just within the front door, at the elevator, he was stopped by an angry woman who screeched at him in Polish.

"And now what are you doing here! Another one who wanders in off the street!"

"Shut up, old woman, or I shall certainly feed you to the barnyard animals," Briggs said in perfect aristocratic Polish, his right eyebrow arching.

She went pale, and she shuffled back a step or two. "Pardon me, sir. A thousand pardons. It's just that I have been having a terrible time with this building."

Briggs turned away from her as the elevator came and he stepped aboard. And he ignored her babbling completely until the doors finally closed and he started up.

If he had been polite, she undoubtedly would have reported him. But this way, she would be too frightened to say anything for fear he was someone important, and she might offend him.

He put his hand in his pocket, and let his fingers curl around the handle of the stiletto which he had taken out before he had entered the building. The elevator doors opened and Phil Smythe was standing by the open door to the apartment.

"Welcome to little Warsaw," he said, stepping aside to let Briggs in. He closed and locked the door. Another man in the apartment turned on the radio fairly loud.

"Bob Townsend, special projects," Smythe introduced them. He and Briggs shook hands.

"Uniform's in the bedroom," Smythe was saying, as he began setting up a slide projector. "We'll go over your papers in a bit. You're Capt. Jan Walcz, born in Warsaw in 1943—right in the middle of the fray. You're an engineer. Mechanical. Your specialty is solid fuel burn structures. As a matter of fact you've done a couple of papers on the subject. Quite good, actually."

"Checkable."

"Perfectly. There is a real Jan Walcz, engineer. We have him on ice for the moment. So you'll be safe."

Townsend had set up the viewing screen, and then he poured Briggs an Irish whiskey and gave it to him.

Briggs smiled. "You're a lifesaver, Townsend," he said. He raised the glass in salute. "Why is it only the bloody British know how to act civilized?"

They all laughed. Then Townsend hit the lights and Smythe turned on the projector. There was a photograph of a very good-looking woman, blond, well-built, on the screen.

"Col. Raya Kasin," Smythe said. "We're offering her up to you as a little bonus."

"Howard and the State Department know anything about this?"

Smythe smiled. "Not a thing. Thought we'd

141

give this to you, one countryman to another. At any rate, the woman is not married. She had a recent affair with one of our people. Could have been a mess, but when we confronted him with the goodies he agreed immediately to cooperate."

"Nasty," Briggs said.

"Filthy. At any rate we've been getting some pretty good stuff from her until recently. The affair has evidently run its course, perhaps brought on by our manipulation, but our man is definitely getting itchy feet, and Raya knows it. On top of that, ten days ago she asked our boy to get her out of the Soviet Union."

"What'd you tell her?"

"Nothing. Not a thing," Townsend broke in. "Her request may be genuine. But she may also have been turned."

"Just like you chaps did with your man."

"Exactly," Townsend said, smiling. He was enjoying this.

She was a good-looking woman, probably in her early thirties. She had high, delicate cheekbones, deep blue eyes, sensuous lips and blond, almost white, hair. She looked very unsual for a Russian.

Smythe flipped to the next slide, the photograph taking away Briggs' breath. It was a cropped picture of two people lying side by side in bed. Nude. Raya Kasin's right leg was thrown over the thigh of a man, most of whose body was cropped out of the photo. Her breasts were small and perfectly formed, her stomach only slightly rounded, and the tuft of pubic hair was platinum blond just as the hair on her head. Her eyes were half closed, her mouth parted to show perfectly white teeth.

"Stunning, isn't she?" Townsend said.

Briggs decided he did not like the man.

Smythe flipped to the next shot, which was a closeup of Raya's face, a man's shoulder above her. They were obviously making love, her features twisted in passion.

Briggs got up. "That's enough, Phil. I'm not a goddamned voyeur."

"You should see the next one . . ." Townsend started, but Briggs cut him off.

"And shut that bloody bastard up, would you."

Townsend glared at him, but said nothing. Smythe advanced quickly through the next half dozen slides, and before Briggs could protest, a photo came up showing the woman dressed in her uniform in a car, coming out of the gate of what appeared to be a military installation. A signboard on the side of the gatehouse was barely legible.

Smythe increased the focus, bringing the signboard closer, until Briggs could read it:

GORKY MISSILE BASE
UNAUTHORIZED VISITORS SHOT ON SIGHT
BY ORDER OF THE COMMANDANT

Briggs whistled, soft and low. "What does she do out there?"

"She's staff liaison officer between base administration and the Department of Missile Defense at the Kremlin."

"Good lord, that's a grade A source, Smythe. And the CIA, State . . . no one knew about it?"

"We passed on the information, of course," Smythe explained. "We just held back on our source."

Briggs was no voyeur, but his mind kept going back to the slide of Raya Kasin lying nude on her back. He was ashamed of himself. "So I'm to take advantage of the fact she's on the rebound—that, and dangle the carrot in front of her nose that we'll get her out."

Smythe nodded.

"Will we?"

"Will we what?"

"Get her out, man. Good Christ, you're not just going to use her, and then toss her aside."

"At this point it's up to you. If getting her out fits with your plans, then so be it. Take her along."

"If it doesn't?"

Smythe shrugged. "We'll cross that bridge when we come to it. Meanwhile you have a job to do."

There were a dozen military vehicles of various types parked behind the apartment building, most of them on loan to the various foreigners who worked in one capacity or another for the Soviet government or military. Briggs, in a Polish Army officer's uniform, polished boots, greatcoat and all, climbed behind the wheel of one of the jeeps, started the engine and took off. No one stopped him, no one challenged him, no one even noticed. If they had, they would have confronted Capt. Jan Walcz, on temporary duty in Moscow. Liaison.

It was well after 3:00 p.m. when he passed the turnoff to Frunze Central Airfield and continued out the main highway toward the west.

They had worked until well after dawn on his own background as well as that of Raya Kasin's. After breakfast Smythe had gone out, and Briggs had managed to get a couple hours sleep. They started again around 10:00 a.m., finally finishing around one, when Briggs got dressed in the uniform.

Before he had left, Smythe had wished him luck, and Townsend apologized for being so brash. "It's just that she's been sort of a class project these months. All of us would have given anything to be in Jerry's shoes. . . ." He clamped it off, realizing he was saying too much.

Driving now, Briggs wondered where the hell Smythe had gotten Townsend. It was men like that who gave the British Secret Intelligence Service such a poor name.

The snow had completely stopped, and the sky was perfectly clear as Briggs sped up once he was clear of the city. There was only an occasional delivery truck on the highway which had been well-plowed. There had been at least eighteen inches of snow, and the wind had piled it into huge drifts. Now it formed high banks on either side of the highway.

He kept thinking about Raya Kasin. There had

been something in her eyes, in the set of her mouth, in the lines of her face, that had intrigued him. Something different about her. Aristocratic, he thought, the way she held herself in the completely candid photographs. He found that he was looking forward to meeting her.

Smythe had managed to get word to her this morning, before she headed out to work at the base, that Briggs would be contacting her with instructions for getting out of the country. According to Smythe she hadn't been at all surprised that help would be coming from a Polish Army officer.

He almost passed the unmarked road that led back to the missile base, and as it was he had to stop and back up. It was after four and the wind was beginning to rise as he headed down the narrow road cut through the thick forest.

About two miles later, he came around a gentle curve, and Gorky Missile Base—one of the Soviet Union's more important defense installations in the Moscow area—came into full view. There were a lot of buildings, some of them obviously barracks, others obviously administration. Many, however, were large, windowless, concrete blockhouses that probably held laboratories or other installations in which secret work was done. The communications center, a large building bristling with antennae and microwave dishes, was off across a clearing to the south. The base was enclosed in a double run of very tall, barbed-wire topped fence, between which were huge loops and rolls of barbed wire. DANGER HIGH VOLT-

AGE signs were posted everywhere. And at one-hundred-yard intervals, large concrete guard towers rose well above the top of the fence.

Briggs took all that in with a glance as he slowed down and approached the main gate. A small sign on the side of the guardhouse read GORKY MISSILE BASE. It was the same gate Raya Kasin had come out of in the photograph.

Two armed guards came out and approached the car as Briggs pulled up and cranked down the window. He had his papers ready, and he handed them up to one of the guards.

"Your name," the guard snapped.

"Capt. Jan Walcz," Briggs said, thickening and slurring his Russian as best he could with a Polish inflection.

The guard nodded, as he examined the papers.

"A Colonel Kasin is expecting me this afternoon," Briggs said helpfully.

The guard looked up, a slight smile playing around the corners of his mouth. "Just one moment, sir," he said. He turned and went back into the guardhouse, as the other guard remained standing off to one side, his weapon at the ready.

It was very cold sitting in the jeep. The wind was starting to kick up the snow, and some of it blew inside. Briggs was about to roll up the window, and say the hell with the guard, when the other one came out of the guardhouse. He was carrying a clipboard, which he handed to Briggs.

"Sign in, please, sir," he said.

Briggs signed his name, rank and serial number, along with the date and the time of entry, and handed the clipboard and pen back up.

The guard checked his signature against the signature in his papers, then handed his things back to him, and nodded for them to open the gate.

"Have you been to Gorky Missile Installation before, sir?"

"No, I have not."

The guard handed him a clip on pass. "Keep this in plain sight, on your lapel, at all times. If you happen to lose it, raise your hands above your head, and remain where you are standing. To do otherwise will probably result in you being shot."

Briggs nodded.

"Colonel Kasin is in building A-17," the guard said. And he turned and pointed it out. It was one of the larger administration buildings, next to one of the blockhouses. "She will be waiting for you at the entry."

"Thank you, comrade," Briggs said.

The guard saluted, Briggs returned it and drove on to the base, his stomach giving a little thrill. It was one thing to penetrate the Soviet border and come into Moscow; it was an entirely different matter to get onto a highly secret and very well-guarded Soviet missile installation.

Col. Raya Kasin was waiting just at the doorway to the administration building when he pulled up, but before he could get out, she came across and climbed in the jeep.

She was a lot taller than he had expected she would be, and much prettier than in the photographs. There was a lot of color in her cheeks from the wind. But she did not look particularly happy.

"Captain Walcz?" she asked.

He nodded. "I'm pleased to meet you Colonel Kasin," he said. They shook hands.

She glanced out the windshield. "We can't talk here or in my office. I told them I was taking you over to the officers' club."

"Are you under suspicion?"

She flinched as if she had been hit. "Everyone is under suspicion, Captain. As a Pole you should know that."

Smythe had not told her the truth about Briggs. But it didn't matter, as long as he could get from her what he had come here for.

He put the jeep in gear and they drove over to the officers' club, where they went inside. At this hour of the afternoon the club was beginning to fill up. Nevertheless they got their vodka and managed a small table in the corner.

When they were settled, and reasonably certain no one was paying them any attention, Raya leaned forward.

"I will do whatever you ask—*whatever*—if you promise to get me out."

Briggs nodded. "How do I know you're not playing a double?"

"I would have turned Jerry in long ago."

"Maybe you already told your people . . ."

"Not my people, you idiot. His. Jerry Landers was giving me secrets from the day we met."

TEN

"He was nothing but a stupid Brit," Raya Kasin explained. "He probably didn't even realize what he was doing until it was too late."

"I thought you were having an affair with him?"

She laughed, the nervous gesture humorless. "I would have had an affair with our pope if it would have helped me get out of here."

Briggs looked at her a little closer. There *was* something different about her. Something . . . not quite Russian. "Are you a countryman?" he asked in Polish.

She smiled, this time it was genuine, if bitter, and she nodded. "I was born in Lódź," she answered in Russian. "And I have no desire to return to Poland. It is worse, from what I am told, than here."

"Where then?"

"Britain. Perhaps Canada, or even the United States."

Briggs took a sip of his drink, then lit a cigarette. She took it from him, so he lit another.

"Tell me about Jerry," he said.

"What about him? I felt sorry for him. He wasn't cut out for this. He's got a wife and kiddies you know. In the end he was getting cold feet. I just wasn't worth it any longer."

"You knew it was coming?"

She nodded.

"So you got him to talk to you. Money in the bank."

She leaned forward. "You're damned right, Walcz, whoever the hell you work for. And I'll use what I learned from Jerry to get me out of here." Her eyes were glistening, and suddenly Briggs realized that a great deal of what she had just said was a sham. She really did have feeling for Landers. Christ.

"Did you ever try to stop him from talking?"

She answered, "Yes," before she realized what she was saying. Then she understood she had ruined that part of it. She nodded. "Yes. But he was like a cossack on a white horse. He wanted to give me trophies."

"I'll get you out, Raya," Briggs said softly. There was no way he was going to leave her here. Goddamned Smythe and his inept crew. Landers was probably another Townsend. If he came face to face with the bastard, Briggs knew he'd do something violent.

There was hope in her eyes when she looked at

him that died with his next words.

"I need some information from you, about this base, first."

"I gave Jerry the hardware list. What do you want now, the organizational chart?"

"I have to know something about a man named Ilya Gamov."

Raya went white, and involuntarily, as if it were a reflex action, she looked around to make sure no one else had heard the question.

"Not here," she hissed, still watching the other officers in the club. "You will have to come to my apartment. We can walk from here, and I can answer your questions."

She rose, an odd expression in her eyes. "You *are* after big game," she said.

Briggs stubbed out his cigarette and followed her out of the officers' club into the darkening afternoon. He hunched up his coat collar as he helped her into the jeep, then got in behind the wheel.

"Gamov is a very big name here, this is practically his own personal installation."

"I was told he is working on some special project here," Briggs said as he drove.

"You are well informed," Raya answered. "Yes, he is. We will talk later. Tonight. Come at ten." She gave him an address out near the planetarium and Moscow City Zoo.

"I'll be there," he said. He stopped in front of her building, and as she was about to get out, he noticed that workers were putting up bunting and red flags on the buildings. "What's going on?" he asked.

152

She followed his gaze, then smiled. "That?" she said. "Our illustrious first party secretary, Comrade Brezhnev, is doing us the honor of coming here tomorrow."

Bingo, Briggs thought. Careful to keep his voice and manner nonchalant, he asked, "Does he come out here often?"

"It's his first time."

"I suppose he'll be here first thing in the morning."

"Late afternoon. About this time, I think," Raya said. Her eyes narrowed. "Why do you ask? Are you after the old man as well as Gamov?"

"No," Briggs said. "I'll see you tonight."

She nodded, then climbed out of the jeep and went into the administration building.

Briggs watched the men working for a minute or two, then headed to the gate, and back to Moscow to set the plan in motion to depose Gamov from his ambitions to the throne.

It was early evening by the time Briggs got back to the Polish apartment, shed his uniform and got dressed again in his civilian clothes, and took a subway across town to Kropotkin's.

He was acutely conscious, now more than ever before, that the clock was ticking on this operation. There were a lot of things to get under control, and less than twenty-four hours in which to make sure everything was ready. Yet he also knew that this kind of opportunity would not present itself again soon.

Gamov was up to something at the base. Brezhnev was on his way out to take a look. Someone again tries to kill the party secretary. Gamov would have to be the chief suspect.

Solchek was going to have to be sacrificed, and Briggs found he did not give a damn. Whatever the man got, he would deserve it. If they took him and his people alive and questioned them, it would sooner or later come out that the entire thing was the idea of Petr Nikolai Solkov, an unidentified member of the KGB . . . of Gamov's directorate. And even if they did not take Solchek and his people alive, Briggs would make sure there was plenty of proof in the building.

When Brezhnev either stepped down or died, Gamov would *not* become the next party secretary.

The bar was particularly crowded this evening, but Solchek's table was half empty. As Briggs started across to him, one of the dissident's friends hurried through the door and directly to Solchek's side. They talked in low voices for a minute or two, and then the man left by the back way.

"You've come back," Solchek laughed, and he motioned for Briggs to take a seat.

"What's going on?" Briggs asked.

Solchek poured Briggs a large glass of cognac and handed it across. "Drink, drink," he said. "Everything is working wonderfully."

"What's going on, Solchek," Briggs repeated. He had a bad feeling about this.

Again the big man laughed. "You asked me to

do something for you—an ingenious something. So now I am doing it."

"Exactly what is it you are doing for me?" Briggs asked, holding himself in check.

"I'm implicating Gamov in a plot to kill the old whoremaster."

"How?"

"By doing exactly as you told me. By following Gamov around and gathering information on him. That, and other things . . ."

"Such as?"

Solchek was enjoying this. "I have friends who are making up certain letters and documents from Gamov to a group we call the Angry Eleven. The papers will be found."

"How soon will you be ready?" Briggs said, finding he didn't give a damn what Solchek was doing. No matter how amateur it was, it would not matter as long as the trail led back to the apartment, and to Petr Nikolai Solkov. He suddenly realized that Esfir was not here.

"Tomorrow, perhaps the next day."

"Where is Esfir?" Briggs asked.

Solchek darkened. "She did not come tonight. She was not feeling well. She missed you."

Briggs held himself in check. Everything within him wanted to leap across the table and take the big man's greasy throat in his hands and squeeze. He wanted to see the man's face turn purple, his eyes pop out, and finally to see him die. Instead, he simply nodded, as if it was of no importance.

"You will have to do it tomorrow afternoon," he said.

Solchek leaned forward. "You have been busy. What did you come up with for us?"

"I was at Gorky this afternoon."

Solchek's eyebrows rose. He was visibly impressed.

"The base practically belongs to Gamov. He's doing something top secret out there, from what I can gather."

Solchek nodded, but held his silence.

"Brezhnev himself is coming out to the base late tomorrow afternoon. They're fixing the place up now for him."

Now Solchek's eyes were bright with excitement. "Tomorrow," he said. He drew inward for several moments, lost in thought.

"Can you be ready by then?"

Solchek nodded. "We will do it, and it will be ironclad. Gamov will be blamed."

"Yes, he will be blamed."

Solchek took a deep drink of his cognac. "And now we will party."

"What information have you gathered on Gamov?" Briggs asked.

"Enough," Solchek said guardedly. "When we cross the border I will give you my little black book."

Briggs took a drink of his cognac, then got to his feet. "I must go out again."

"Will I see you before . . . tomorrow afternoon?"

"Possibly not."

"If something goes wrong . . . if there is, shall I say, a need for haste, I shall meet you at the place where you picked up the car.''

Briggs nodded.

''Have you a plan for me?''

''Yes, I do,'' Briggs said, with only the smallest of twinges for his lie, and he turned on his heel and left the bar.

He wanted to go back to Solchek's apartment to check on Esfir, he was worried about her. But it was nearing ten, and it was crucial that he not miss his appointment with Raya Kasin. Briggs had figured he would have a large problem getting onto the base at Gorky, and then coming up with the information on Gamov's activities there that Howard had wanted. But with the help of Smythe and of the chance situation with Raya Kasin and a British embassy employee, it had been easy . . . so far.

Briggs caught a subway that went under the river, and across town to the zoo, which was only a block and a half from Raya Kasin's apartment complex.

There were at least two dozen huge, ten-story apartment buildings scattered across a treeless field. They looked like gigantic toy blocks stuck in the snow, the lights on in the various apartments making a checkerboard pattern against the dark night sky.

He showed up at her apartment building door a few minutes after ten, and she was waiting for him.

''I didn't think you were coming,'' she said, stepping out from the shadows in the front hallway. The corridor light was out.

"Sorry I'm late," Briggs said. He took her arm as they went outside. She stuffed her hands in her coat pockets, and turned onto a path behind the building that went down a shallow hill toward a frozen creek at the bottom.

"The children in the apartment use this place to slide down on. I brought some cardboard from the base for them to use. I am the popular one of the building for now." She laughed.

"When did you see Jerry Landers last?" Briggs asked.

She looked up at him, her eyes slightly moist. "Last week," she said. "But we are not walking to discuss him, but to discuss Comrade Gamov."

"What is he working on at Gorky?" Briggs asked.

"Not many people know, for sure, but he trusts me," she said. And now her laugh was bitter.

"You know him?"

"I have been decoration at his dacha. He has parties. He . . ."

"He what?" Briggs prompted.

"He is not a lover of women . . . in fact I think he despises us."

"Then why were you invited to his dacha?"

"There are a lot of women there at his parties. All of them young and very good-looking. All of them willing to . . . sleep with whoever might be there."

It all came clear to Briggs. Gamov's methods were old, but nonetheless effective. "They . . . do this there, at Gamov's dacha?"

"Certainly?"

"And you?"

She shook her head violently. "He asked me, but the first two times I was out there I made excuses. After that he left me alone. I think he wanted me there though as decoration."

"And yet you kept going back?"

She stopped and looked up into Briggs' eyes. "One does not refuse a man so powerful as Gamov. He is KGB and very close to Party Secretary Brezhnev himself." After a moment or two, they continued down the hill, and then along the creek.

"You said not many people knew what he was up to out at the base. Do you?"

"Yes . . . or at least some of it," Raya Kasin said. "It has to do with automatic warfare."

"I don't understand," Briggs said.

"If we are attacked, our missiles will be sent off of their own accord," she said. "Or if there is some crisis . . something that happens anywhere in the world, that significantly increases the probability of a first strike, our missiles would be launched."

"Who determines the probability?"

"The Central Computer Center."

Briggs stopped her. "You mean to tell me that Gamov is tying the Soviet missile force into a computer that will launch a war whenever it thinks there's a threat?"

"From what I understand," Raya Kasin said, nodding. "He spoke of the system as a gigantic chess computer. We have the machine now that will beat our own masters. Of course it was they who programmed it in the first place. But isn't war nothing more than a gigantic chess game, with seemingly endless possibilities . . . millions of strategies?''

It was monstrous. Worse, it was insane.

"How far along is he with his . . . project?''

"I'm not sure. He's been working at for a year now.''

"Just at Gorky?''

"No. At our missile installations all across the country, from what I can gather.''

"Does Brezhnev know?''

"No one knows for sure what's happening.''

"But you do?''

"Not completely. A lot of what I'm saying is just guesswork. Jerry first asked me about it, otherwise I wouldn't have paid any attention. Then I was hired as liaison between the base and the Military Affairs Department at the Politboro Support Center, and I learned about Gamov's 'inspection' trips to our missile installations.''

Something else was bothering Briggs. "What about Gorky Missile Base? If it's just another installation, why is Gamov spending so much time there? Why is it his pet base?''

"The central computer is located there.''

They had come to a sharp bend in the small creek, over which several thick willow trees had grown, blocking their progress unless they crossed to the other side.

"Why do you suppose Brezhnev is coming out to Gorky tomorrow? Does he know what Gamov has been up to?''

"I don't think so. But I think Gamov is going to tell him tomorrow."

"It's ready?"

She nodded. "I think so. I think tomorrow Brezhnev will have a private showing, and then later everyone else will get the chance."

They turned and started back toward the apartment building. It was very cold, below zero, and the wind was beginning to kick up again, bringing the wind chill factor even lower.

"How long have you been here, in Moscow?" Briggs asked.

"Twelve years," she said. "I joined the army when I was sixteen. We were very poor. It was my only way out. I was sent here to school at the university just after my boot camp, and I went to work immediately."

"You made rank quickly."

"Because I slept with the right men!" she retorted bitterly. "I've not been poor since I arrived here. But now I'm tired . . . sick to death of it all." She shook her head, tears again coming to her eyes. "I'm twenty-eight years old, and I feel like a burned-out old lady. It's not fair."

Briggs had stuffed his hands in his pockets, but he again took her arm, and helped her up the shallow hill. He was in a quandary. He wanted to help her, he wanted to get her out, and yet he did not know if he could trust her enough to warn her about tomorrow afternoon. Whatever Solchek and his people did, however they pulled off the bogus assassination attempt, all hell would break loose on that base. All hell would break loose across the country, but especially at that base.

It was possible that in the confusion that would follow such an attempt, she might be able to slip away, but it was more likely that the base would be sealed tighter than a drum.

In the end, of course, he understood that it would be criminal to possibly sacrifice the mission. Yet . . .

"Do you have an office at the Kremlin? Or do you spend most of your time at the base?" Briggs asked.

"About half and half," she said. "It's why I have an apartment here in the city. I also have a room in the BOQ on base."

"Stay in your Kremlin office tomorrow. Give yourself an ironclad excuse."

She stopped, startled. "What are you saying to me, Walcz?"

"Don't go out to Gorky tomorrow. Stay here in the city. I can't tell you any more than that."

Her mind was racing, he could see it in her eyes. "Something is going to happen to Brezhnev? Is Gamov going to assassinate him?"

It was Briggs' turn to be startled. "What gave you that idea?"

She shrugged. "Gamov wants to be first party secretary. Everyone knows that."

"Would he resort to assassination?" Briggs asked. Christ, this setup was perfect.

Again she shrugged. "Who knows. Gamov is a strange man."

"Don't go to Gorky tomorrow."

"All right," she said. "And afterwards? For my help?"

"I will get you out of the Soviet Union. Wait here at your door at ten o'clock for the next several nights. I will come for you."

Briggs took the subway back across town, and got off between Kropotkin's and Solchek's apartment. For just a moment he hesitated there, one part of him knowing he should return to Solchek to find out what the hell the dissident was planning for tomorrow, while the other part felt compelled to go back to the apartment and see if he could find Esfir.

The choice was easy. Ten minutes later he was hurrying down the slope to the apartment building, where he took the stairs two at a time to the fifth floor.

He listened at Solchek's door for a long time, but heard nothing. He knocked softly, and when there was no answer he tried the knob. It was locked. He pulled out his stiletto, the long, slender blade gleaming in the harsh light from a single bulb down the corridor, and within seconds had the lock undone, and was entering the apartment.

He closed and locked the door then stood in the dark living room for a while, letting his eyes adjust. Only a very small amount of light came through the windows from outside.

The apartment smelled of cabbage, and something else he could not quite define, it was so faint, although he was certain it was an odor he knew.

He moved silently across the living room, past

the kitchen. No one was there. The main bedroom door was closed. Briggs opened it slowly, and the faint odor came stronger. His stomach flipped over as he suddenly recognized what it was.

Briggs groped for the light switch, flipped it on, and his eyes automatically went to the bed.

Esfir lay face down on the bed in a huge stain of her own blood, the metallic odor strong now. Her entire back, and the backs of her legs were nothing but raw meat.

There was blood on the floor as well, and splattered up on the walls.

Briggs moved carefully to the side of the bed, and took Esfir's wrist in his hand to check her pulse, but immediately dropped it. Her body was cold and stiff. She had been dead for at least six hours.

He turned and left the apartment. Downstairs in his own apartment, he hid his KGB identification, as well as the big automatic, then slipped out of the building, only one thought on his mind . . . Solchek's death.

ELEVEN

The weather was intensely cold, although another front was developing over Finland, and would make its way here to Moscow in a few days. There would be much warmer temperatures, but they would pay the penalty with more snow.

Gamov shrugged. When it came to things of that nature he was a fatalist. For anything else, he demanded perfection.

Reza was waiting outside the control frame vault of the main computer when Gamov stepped through the doorway. The heavy metal door closed with a dull thud, and the electronic lock cycled.

Gamov was pleased. His system, which he called Western Watchdog, was ready to come on line. The computer had worked out scenario after scenario—sending out the missiles on some, holding back on others—with faultless precision.

Once it was put in service, they need never worry again about Western threats of aggression. Everyone in the world would know that war was now out of the hands of mere human beings.

Gamov had to chuckle at his own joke. What it meant, in reality, was that the United States and NATO would not even be able to make the slightest of threatening gestures, for fear the hair-trigger computer would send its missiles.

It was delicious, Gamov thought, smiling at Reza. With Western Watchdog in place, and with himself as first party secretary, the world would soon belong to the Soviet Union.

Reza looked at his watch. "It is almost time, sir," he said.

"When I explained some of this to him the other night, the old fool practically salivated," Gamov said half under his breath. No one but Reza was in hearing range. "He had to come out and see it. It won't be long now, Reza, not long now."

They donned their thick coats, fur hats and gloves, and with the dozen or so other men in their party, including the base commander, an obsequious little man, left the control center, and rode in a heated bus to the main gate where one hundred troops were lined up in military precision despite the sub-zero weather.

There, they got off the bus, and lined up by the speakers' platform.

Reza held back, and raised a walkie-talkie to his lips. He said something into it, and a moment later he was evidently answered, because he looked up, then strode to where Gamov and the others stood waiting.

"His party has just turned off the highway. They are on their way."

Gamov started to turn toward the base commander, when the sound of an explosion, followed by the sharp clatter of automatic weapons fire came to them from up the road.

For several long seconds they all seemed frozen into a tableau of stunned, frightened men.

Gamov was the first to snap out of it, and he began issuing orders. Within moments, the honor guard were piling onto the bus, and were headed up the road. Seconds later, a siren began to sound, and a dozen jeeps all bearing soldiers streamed through the main gate.

Reza was busy on the walkie-talkie, relaying Gamov's orders.

Two hundred troops hurriedly ringed the computer control center, the main gate was closed, and a helicopter came up from the airstrip and landed twenty-five yards from the main gate.

Gamov, Reza and the base commander hurried to the machine, climbed aboard, and they lifted off, swinging wide of the entry road.

Immediately they could see fierce fighting going on near the wreckage of two limousines, and three jeeps. A group of what appeared to be ragtag civilians were firing down on the troops from a thick stand of trees at the intersection of the highway and the base access road. Farther back up the highway, about a half mile from the fighting were several automobiles, and one truck. All were pointed toward Moscow.

The helicopter pilot, an expert, banked low over the action, making certain he was always moving fast and constantly changing direction.

As they watched, two of the rebels went down, and several others were hidden in a thick puff of smoke as two or more hand grenades went off simultaneously in their immediate vicinity.

Gamov found himself looking down at the struggle with an air of detachment. Brezhnev was probably dead. At least it appeared so from the looks of the two limousines. Both were riddled with bullet holes, and one of them lay on its side, on fire. Yet Gamov found he didn't realy care. If Brezhnev were dead, then the struggle as to who would take over now would fall between himself and Andropov. And unless something had happened to change Brezhnev's mind over the past few days, the first party secretary would have recommended Gamov as his successor.

Andropov would fight that decision, no doubt, so the struggle was not over with yet. In a strange way, Gamov felt glad that the fight would now be joined. One way or the other this would be finished in the next twenty-four to forty-eight hours.

Five of the rebels broke away and raced toward the highway, where they had parked their vehicles. Meanwhile, thirty or forty troops from the base had raced up the access road, and were waiting now on the highway for the rebels to emerge from the woods.

"Around," Gamov shouted. "Come around, I

don't want to miss this!''

The helicopter slewed sickeningly to the left and then in a tight arc to the right, coming up and hovering over the intersection of the highway and the access road as the rebels broke out of the woods.

They never had a chance. They didn't even fire a single shot. Meanwhile, the last of the rebels back in the woods went down or were blown to pieces, and it was over.

Gamov directed the pilot to set them down on the road opposite the wreckage of the two limousines. When they were down, he and Reza and the base commander jumped out and hurried to the two big black cars, as the medical units arrived.

Leonid Brezhnev was dead. His body bullet-ridden. His eyes open.

Gamov stared at his body for several long moments, the thought occurring to him that at least the man's head and face were intact. He would look good for the State funeral.

Another thought struck him as well. None of this could get out. It would be disastrous to their image worldwide if it came out that hooligans had defeated the Russian Army, and had assassinated the first party secretary.

Even Andropov would agree, Gamov thought. Brezhnev had been in failing health. The entire world had seen that. He had not appeared in public now for some weeks. Last night he had simply died in his sleep. A fittingly gentle end for a great leader.

* * *

Briggs had not rested very much in the last eighteen hours. From Esfir's deathbed, he had gone to Smythe's Polish apartment in the foreign section, where he had remained, through the rest of that night, and through the day, waiting for word as to what happened.

Smythe had agreed that Briggs' only option at this point was to remain well clear of the operation. If it went well, then good, it would be time for him to make his way home. If it had gone sour, at least he would not be in the way when the chips began to fall.

Yes, all during his brief, self-imposed exile, he could not help but think of Esfir versus Raya. One was uncertain, the other self-assured. One naïve, used; the other a realist, a user. Yet neither of them deserved the life that had been imposed on them. No one did.

During this brief, but intense time, Briggs also thought about Gamov and about Solchek. In each case he felt himself go loose—he felt himself drop into mental gear for combat. There were two men in the world at this moment on whom he wanted to inflict bodily harm. And they were Gamov and Solchek. Two men at opposite ends of the Russian scale . . . but both of them cut from essentially the same immoral cloth.

It was well after seven o'clock, long past dark, when Townsend came back to the apartment. Briggs by that point was hyper, and he waited just around the corner from the door, his stiletto at the ready.

When Townsend came in, flicked on the light

and turned so that he could suddenly see Briggs standing there, his complexion went pale, and he stumbled.

"Oh," he said.

Briggs relaxed, and put the stiletto away. "What is it? What happened?"

"Christ, you scared me," Townsend swore.

"What the hell happened?" Briggs snapped. He was at the raw edge.

"You were standing there, and . . ."

Briggs grabbed the man by his lapels. "What the hell happened out at Gorky?"

"You haven't heard?" Townsend asked, incredulously. His eyes went automatically to the radio on the table.

"I haven't listened to the radio. What the hell happened?"

"They got him, for God's sake! They killed Brezhnev!"

"What?"

"At least that's what we surmise. Tass is saying Brezhnev died in his sleep last night. But of course we saw him leave his dacha and head out for Gorky. They say it was his heart."

"But we know better."

"That's right," Townsend said.

Briggs went into the bedroom where he grabbed his coat and hat and pulled them on. Townsend had followed him in.

"I can only assume that you've gotten what you can from Gorky, so now it's time for you to get out. Phil wanted to know if you'd need transportation, or if the Cousins had provided it for you?"

Briggs pushed past the man, ignoring him and headed to the front door.

"I don't know who the hell you think you are, but we went through a lot of trouble for you, mister," Townsend shouted.

Briggs paused at the front door. Brezhnev was dead. Solchek's people had killed him. Now all hell was going to break loose, and Townsend was playing personalities with him. He was going to have to speak to Sir Roger about this one.

"Where's Jerry Landers?" Briggs asked softly.

Townsend's eyes widened. "What?"

"Jerry Landers. What did you do with him?"

"Don't talk to me about it . . ." Townsend started, but then he thought better of it. "Smythe sent him home. He left this afternoon. Early."

"Good," Briggs said. "If I had run into the sonofabitch, I would have killed him." He turned and left the apartment.

The wind blew in fitful gusts as Briggs strode across the parking lot and down the three blocks to the subway station where he took a train across town, back to the neighborhood between Kropotkin's and Solchek's apartment.

A civil police car, followed by two Army jeeps raced by, their blue lights flashing, their sirens screaming.

For a while, Briggs held back in the shadows. He had a fair idea where they were going. But he had to be certain, so he headed carefully up the street toward Solchek's apartment building, making sure that he was not being followed, and that no one was paying any attention to him.

A number of people had gathered, in respectful silence, on the road above the apartment building. Every light in the place was on, and there were policemen and soldiers everywhere.

Whatever had exactly happened this afternoon out at Gorky, it certainly had been tied to Solchek. Very soon if not already, they would be finding the Petr Nikolai Solkov KGB identification and weapon he had left in the fourth floor apartment. It would provide another link to Gamov.

After a while, Briggs turned and left, heading back toward Kroptokin's. He had a fair idea where Solchek would be at this moment . . . huddled and afraid. But he wanted to make absolutely certain he didn't make a mistake and miss the man. This was one appointment he definitely was looking forward to making.

As he walked, mindless of the cold, only aware of his surroundings, he was taken back to his days as a young man in Soho. They had trained him well, the emigrés: They had trained him how to stalk, how to be invisible in a city, how to kill, how to avoid being captured or killed. Hour after hour, month after month, for years, the lessons had been drummed into his head. Letter drops, radio techniques, tailing, being tailed. The entire gamut of espionage trade craft—the experience of dozens of men and women who had worked for the best secret services in the world, under the worst, most trying conditions. The ones who had survived, the true experts, had been the ones to teach Briggs.

The streets surrounding Kropotkin's were completely blocked off by military jeeps and civil police units, so Briggs did not even try to get closer. If Solchek had been back at the apartment or here at the bar, he would have been caught. In which case it would be too late for Briggs to do anything about it.

But he didn't think the big dissident would have let himself be taken that easily. Their plan evidently was pulled off—Brezhnev was dead—but just as evident was the fact that something had gone wrong. Someone had been captured, and the trail had come back to Solchek and his hangouts. If the big dissident understood that, he would have run to his bolthole. The place where Briggs had gotten the car to drive out to Gamov's dacha. Solchek would be there. Waiting. Hiding. Cowering in the darkness.

There was the possibility, of course, that the police knew about the car as well, and were there now. It was very possible that, between the apartment, Kropotkin's, and the car place, Solchek was arrested. But, as he hurried through the frozen night, Briggs sincerely hoped the man was still free. Just a little longer.

It took him less than twenty minutes to make it to the garage. He stopped a half block away, and studied the building. There was only one window lit in the apartment above, and no movement. There was no traffic, no pedestrians, nothing. The street and all the buildings on it (mostly commercial establishments, such as electrical shops, and plumbing businesses) were dark, except for the one light above the garage.

After a while, Briggs pushed away from where he was standing, crossed the street and walked quickly down to the garage, where he tried to door. It was unlocked, so he slipped inside, after first pulling out his stiletto. He closed the door, plunging the interior of the garage into darkness.

He could smell the odor of oil and gasoline from the car, and he moved a couple of feet forward, until he bumped into the low rear bumper with his shins and stopped, every one of his senses attuned to the interior of the garage, attuned to detect the presence of another human being.

And he did—he smelled cognac. Faintly, but there nevertheless.

He moved softly to the left, around the side of the car to the front door. Slowly, carefully, making as little noise as possible, he eased the door handle down, and opened the door. The dome light was not working. He reached inside and found the headlight switch, and pulled it on.

The garage was suddenly flooded with yellow light. Solchek, bundled in a thick parka, a cloth cap on his head, a thick woolen scarf around his neck, stood with his back to the far corner of the garage. He held a pistol in his right hand.

"It's me," Briggs said, stepping around to the front of the car. He held the stiletto down at his side so that it was hidden from view in the folds of his heavy coat.

"I've been waiting here all afternoon," Solchek said. "Brezhnev is dead."

"I know," Briggs said, passing in front of the car, and slowly edging toward the big man. "The military and the police are at your apartment, and at Kropotkin's. They're looking for you."

"They'll never find me," Solchek said. "Not alive. Nor am I leaving here with you."

Briggs smiled. Solchek's swallowing of the KGB cover was just another link in the chain.

"It was a setup all the time. You wanted to get something on me, so that you could put me away."

"If I wanted something on you, it would be the abuse and murder of an innocent girl."

"She was nothing but a slut," Solchek bellowed.

"An innocent young girl, whom you used mercilessly."

"She was a whore," Solchek screamed. "She slept with you!"

Briggs had been moving slowly forward all this time, and now he was practically on top of the man. He could smell, in addition to the cognac, the odor of fear and sweat. Solchek was trembling, his eyes wide, his nostrils flared, and flecks of spittle on his lips.

"What did you want?" the dissident cried. "What did you want with me? What did I ever do to you?" He tried to back farther into the corner, but when he could not, he suddenly raised the pistol, at Briggs' chest, cocking the hammer back.

Briggs knocked the gun aside, and it went off. At that same moment he brought the stiletto up in a short, vicious arc, the razor-sharp blade easily

176

penetrating the man's heavy coat. The blade deflected off one of Solchek's ribs, puncturing a lung, instead of his heart, and he shoved out with all of his might, knocking Briggs off balance for the moment.

Briggs fell back against the hood of the car, as Solchek again brought the pistol up. He just managed to duck beneath the gun when it went off, and he drove upwards, the image of Esfir's abused, bloody body lying on the bed filling his mind. With his left hand, he drove Solchek's head up and back, exposing his neck, and with his right, drove the stiletto to the hilt into the man's windpipe, then violently jerked it to the left, severing several major arteries, including the carotid.

He managed to leap back out of the way as blood spurted from the massive wound, and Solchek struggled for a moment then fell to his knees, crumpling in a heap on his side.

The gunshots would have been heard. Someone would be here very soon.

Briggs wiped the blade on Solchek's parka, then sheathed it. Bending down beside the body, he took the man's index finger on his right hand, dipped it in a pool of his own blood on the front of his coat, and in the concrete floor wrote the ragged letters: G A M O V, letting the last letter slide as if it had been the last thing the man had written before he died.

Then Briggs shut off the car light, and at the door peered outside. There was no one there. No lights had come on. No one had come out to investigate.

He slipped out of the garage, closing the door behind him, and hurried down the street without looking back.

Six blocks away from the garage, he ducked down into a subway tunnel (after first making sure he had wiped off what little of Solchek's blood he had gotten on his sleeve) and took the next train across town to the zoo.

There weren't many people on the train, and no one paid him much attention. He had made sure he would not be dressed too shabbily, or too fine. He looked now like nothing more than the average Muscovite on his way home. Perhaps an office worker, a bookkeeper, or a small business manager. He let his face reflect that boredom and tiredness, so that overall he presented a totally unremarkable picture, despite the fact his heart was hammering and inside he was in turmoil.

He had killed a man. Although he had gone to the rendezvous with the man with the intention of killing him, for what he was and what he had done to an innocent girl, it still was murder, and Briggs was not particularly proud of himself.

He knew every man he had ever killed. He knew their faces, and especially the expression on their eyes when they were dying. Often, their faces haunted his dreams. He hated it. He hated what his life had become, even though he knew that his existence—and the existence of men like him—was necessary.

Christ, he told himself. He had done nothing tonight to be proud of. Nothing in his life, for that matter, to which he could point with pride as his achievement. Christ!

Incredibly (considering all that had happened this evening) it was still before 10:00 p.m. when Briggs showed up at Raya Kasin's apartment building. The corridor was deserted—she had not yet come down to the front door to wait for him.

Instead, he took the back stairs up, two at a time, to the seventh floor. He was just stepping out of the stairway when Raya Kasin was coming out of her apartment.

She stopped, startled, when she saw him. Her complexion was very pale, her eyes wide. She was obviously very frightened.

He hurried down the corridor to her. "We can't leave yet," he said softly. "Is there anyone in your apartment?"

She shook her head, unable to speak for the moment. He took her arm, and could feel that she was trembling.

"We have to talk," Briggs said.

After several long seconds, she finally nodded, unlocked her apartment door and they went inside. Finland and freedom were such a long ways away at this moment, Briggs thought. But there was one last thing he was going to have to do before they left. It was a change in the scenario . . . the most dangerous change of all . . . but Briggs knew that he would not be able to allow himself to leave until it was done.

TWELVE

Raya Kasin's apartment was a lot smaller, and somewhat less homey, than Solchek's, yet it contained many of the luxury items that her rank allowed her to afford, including a washer and dryer and a television set. But the place seemed devoid of any personal touches. It could have been the barracks apartment of any of a thousand officers. There were no photographs, only one painting, and no other bits of bric-a-brac. It was the apartment of a very lonely woman.

"He's dead. He was ambushed just off the highway near the base," Raya said when they were inside and she had locked the door.

"I didn't have anything to do with it."

"But you knew! You warned me to stay away. You knew it was coming!"

"No, I didn't," Briggs said. They stood facing each other across the living room. "I knew something might happen out there, but not that."

"Who did it?"

"Gamov . . . rather, his people caused it."

"Gamov. He's to be our first party secretary now?"

Briggs came across the room to her. "We cannot allow that to happen, Raya. He cannot become the leader of the Soviet government. It would mean war."

"What do you care?" she asked sharply. "Poland is already a satellite state."

"I'm not Polish," he said.

She stared at him, then nodded. "What are you, KGB? Have I dug my grave?"

"I'm not KGB."

"What then?" she shouted.

Briggs took her by the shoulders, and in the next instant she collapsed into his arms, shaking and crying. She was very frightened.

As he comforted her he could not help but think of the differences and the similarities between her and Esfir. Both shared the common malady of being lost souls. He had felt sorry for Esfir, and now he felt an equal concern for Raya. Yet he needed her.

After a long while, she began to calm down. He took out his handkerchief and dried her tears.

"It's silly of me," she said, attempting to smile through her fear. "Colonels aren't supposed to cry."

"I'm going to get you out of the country, I promise you that. But first I'm going to need your help with something."

"Is it important?" she asked, looking at him through wide eyes.

"Vitally."

She nodded after a second.

Briggs had to ask himself if he thought she would be able to do it. If she would be able to hold up. But then he realized that he had no other viable choice at this point.

"You told me that you knew Gamov. That you've been to his dacha."

"Parties," she said. "But his people were already here."

"His people?"

"He heads an investigatory committee. His people were here asking me about what happened at the base."

"What did you tell them?"

"Nothing," she replied, an edge of hysteria to her voice. "What could I have told them?"

"I have to get out to Gamov's dacha. Tonight. I must see him."

"Why? What have you got to say to? . . ." She stopped, then backed away from him. "You're going to kill him."

"He cannot become first party secretary."

"Who then? Kosygin? Andropov?"

"Anyone but Gamov."

"I . . ." she started, but again she lost the words.

"Can you telephone him? Will he believe that you must see him. This evening yet?"

"What are you then?" she asked. "Is it true? Are you going to kill Gamov as you killed

Brezhnev?'' She looked away, but Briggs reached out and gently turned her head back.

"I was sent here to stop an evil man from taking control of the Soviet Union. If Gamov gains control, there would certainly be a war . . . a war from which no one would escape.''

"You're an American," Raya said in amazement.

"Actually not," Briggs said, impatiently. "Will you help me?''

"Yes," Raya said after the briefest of hesitations. "To kill Gamov, I think almost everyone in Russia would agree to help you.''

Gamov was beside himself with anger. He thumped the armrest in the back seat of his limousine, impatient now to get to his dacha. Reza was driving—at this juncture he was the only man Gamov could trust.

Andropov had not even shown up at the briefing room. He had stayed away. Nor had he made a single comment against the so-called evidence that had begun to pile up.

Yet Gamov had not expected anything other than what was happening right now. This was the fight he knew would occur the moment Brezhnev died . . . no matter how he died. But assassination?

"Hurry," he shouted.

"Yes, comrade," Reza replied softly, and the big Zil limousine sped up slightly.

They wanted a fight, they'd get one, Gamov

thought. He had enough tapes now in his safe to bring nearly the entire Soviet hierarchy down to its knees. He did not think he'd actually have to use the material; just its threat would be enough to bring the Politburo into line.

It had been nearly ten o'clock by the time they had gotten out of the center, and now it was past 10:30 as they pulled off the main highway and raced up the long driveway to the manned gate a half mile down from the house.

As they came around the final curve, Reza slowed way down, and they pulled to a halt. The gate guards, recognizing the car, came out nevertheless to visually check Gamov in the back seat.

Gamov cranked down the rear window. The guard cautiously approached.

"Has anyone been here tonight?" Gamov shouted.

"No, sir," the guard replied.

"No one has come through this gate this evening?"

"No, comrade, no one."

The gate swung open, and Gamov cranked his window back up, and directed Reza to proceed. He felt somewhat relieved. He had half expected Andropov to send his people out here to look around. He would not have put it past the man.

Reza pulled up at the front entrance to the house, but even before he had a chance to get out, Gamov had jerked open his own door, and raced up the walk and inside.

Provnenko, the duty guard shift captain, jumped up from his table in the central hall, as

Gamov strode across the corridor. Reza was right behind him.

"Has anyone been here? Have there been any calls?" Gamov shouted.

"Yes, comrade. There has been a telephone call."

Gamov had been heading for the stairs, but he stopped in his tracks, and looked around at Reza, then at the duty officer.

"Who called me?"

"Colonel Kasin, comrade. Just a few minutes ago."

"What did this colonel want with me?"

"I don't know, comrade. She said it was vitally important she speak with you. She said it concerned Gorky."

Gamov could feel his blood pressure rising. "She said that? On an open line?" he screamed.

Provnenko stepped back a pace. "Yes, comrade."

"Who is this officer?" Gamov shouted, turning to Reza. "Find out who she is."

"Begging your pardon, Comrade. But I took the liberty of doing that."

Gamov spun on him. "Well?"

"She is the Kremlin liaison officer for the base."

Gamov had the image of a mousy-looking blond woman. He remembered her now. No threat. Absolutely none. She was Polish he seemed to remember.

"What did she want?"

"I don't know, comrade. She said it was urgent."

Gamov turned to Reza. "Telephone the slut. Find out what it is she wants. Then come up."

Reza inclined his head slightly, and Gamov went up the stairs, taking them two at a time. He hurried to his private chambers, where he slammed the door, then threw off his overcoat, uniform blouse, and loosened his tie. At the sideboard he poured himself a stiff vodka, tossed it down, then poured himself another.

Across the room, in his dressing room, he took off his tie, and then his shoes, and slipped into a smoking jacket and slippers.

He took his drink down the corridor and into his study, where he opened the large safe behind his desk, pulled out the brown leather volume which contained the index of his videotape file, then sat down.

No one could touch him now. Nothing could sway the course of events which would as surely put him in the office of the first party secretary as the sun would rise tomorrow.

He felt smug. But then he had a right to feel that way, he told himself. When it was over, he would have pulled off the greatest coup ever conceived.

He sipped his drink and was lighting a cigarette when Reza came in. There was an odd, almost wistful look on the man's face. It was almost frightening.

"I spoke with Colonel Kasin," he said.

"Well?" Gamov snapped.

"I asked her to come out here."

"You what?" Gamov started to complain, but

then he *did* remember the woman. He had invited her out here on several occasions for parties, his video cameras rolling. But she had never participated . . . never really participated. The bitch.

"She says she has information that is vital to your immediate future," Reza continued.

Gamov's eyes narrowed. "And what else?"

"That's all. I told her to come out here immediately. She said she was bringing another officer. Someone who used to work for the Komitet."

"Andropov. It must be one of his people. It has to be! Alert the front gate. I want them both searched," Gamov said. "Strip searched."

Reza nodded, left the study and went downstairs to the duty officer's table, where he picked up the phone, and dialed for the front gate.

"There will be two officers coming here this evening," he said without needing to identify himself. "One is Col. Raya Kasin. The other is her guest. They are to be let through without question."

The gate guard asked if they should be searched.

Reza looked down at Provnenko and smiled. "No," he said. "That will not be necessary."

"How will we get clear?" Raya was asking as they left the city in her small civilian car. "As soon as they find . . . Gamov, they'll come after us."

"They'll expect us to run to the nearest border. We won't."

"How will we get out?" There was a slight touch of hysteria to Raya's voice.

"Don't worry about it," Briggs said, but he was. The MiG waiting for him near the Finland border was a one-seater. There was no room for Raya. Yet he knew that he could not leave her behind. Nor could he let Gamov find a possible way out of his difficulties. The man could not become the new Soviet leader. It would be disastrous.

She was right though. As soon as Gamov's body was discovered, any chance of escape they might have would be cut off.

But the odds had been worse before. The first step was Gamov. When that was accomplished, he would worry about getting them out of here. There always was a way.

Raya was driving, and from time to time she glanced over at him. She could see that there was a slight grin on his lips, and it seemed to upset her.

"This is just a lark for you, isn't it?" she said.

"No it's not, Raya. Far from it."

"Then what are you grinning for? Are you crazy?" Her eyes were wide. She was starting to work herself up. Briggs reached over and held her arm.

"Easy," he said. "We haven't lost yet, have we?"

Her eyes were shiny. But she managed to shake her head. "Not yet," she said.

The temperature continued to drop, and away from the relative protection of the city the wind had begun to kick up again. As he had on more than one occasion recently, Briggs thought about California and the work he had done there for several years. Although he hadn't been content in Hollywood producing low budget movies, he had been happy from time to time. Happy and warm and out of physical danger.

They passed the turnoff that led to the back road into Gamov's dacha, and Briggs sat a little straighter in his seat.

Raya had said Gamov's guests were never searched, and he had guessed the man probably had an X-ray setup, like at airports, to screen everyone coming in. But Raya disagreed.

"He has a monumental arrogance," she had said earlier. "He has guards all over the place, but they're mostly for show. He relies on the fact that he is a very important man . . . too important to attack."

Nevertheless, Briggs had unstrapped his stiletto and sheath when Raya was not watching, and hidden the weapon beside his seat. If they were stopped and searched at the gate, at least he'd have a chance of getting through without the stiletto being detected.

If need be, he told himself grimly, he'd kill Gamov with his bare hands.

At length they came to the turnoff that led up to Gamov's dacha, and Raya slowed down, almost as if she could not bring herself to go on. Before Briggs could say anything, however, she made the turn, and sped up, coming apparently to another resolve.

"The main gate is just up here a little ways,"

she said softly.

"Easy," Briggs said.

She glanced at him. It was very dark here amidst the forest that tightly crowded the narrow road.

"When we get to the house, I want you to park the car facing out, and leave the keys in the ignition."

She nodded.

"Don't be surprised by anything I say or do in there, either."

"What do you mean by that?" she asked nervously.

"Whatever happens, pretend you know what's going on. My real name is Anatoli Baturin, KGB, Special Investigations Department. My most recent cover was as Jan Walcz, a Polish officer sent to investigate the goings on at Gorky Missile Base."

"And who did you work for?"

"Yuri Andropov," Briggs said.

They came around the last curve, and Raya pulled to a halt at the gate. Two guards came out as she cranked down her window, and held out her identification.

"Colonel Kasin," she snapped.

The guard looked from the ID to Raya's face, then to Briggs'. He nodded. "Drive directly to the house. Park in front. You will be met."

The gate swung open, and the guard stepped back. Raya put the car in gear and drove through.

Briggs pocketed his stiletto in its sheath, as they came up to the large house. "No matter what happens, do exactly as I say," he said.

She nodded, pulling up, dousing the lights and switching off the ignition. She left the keys, and she and Briggs got out of the car and walked up to the front door, which was opened for them by a thin, dark, very good-looking young man.

"Colonel Kasin?" the man asked.

Raya nodded and reached for her identification, but the dark man stopped her. "That will not be necessary." He turned to Briggs. "And you, comrade?"

"I would prefer to reveal my identity only to Comrade Gamov. I have something of very great importance for his ears only."

The dark man bowed slightly. "As you wish, comrade. But I am Reza Makat, Comrade Gamov's private secretary and aidé-de-camp."

Briggs said nothing. After a moment, Reza nodded again and led them past the duty officer's position, Provnenko gone now on a useless errand, and up the stairs to Gamov's study.

"Please have a seat," Reza said. "Comrade Gamov will be with you momentarily." He backed out of the room and closed the door.

As soon as he was gone, Raya was about to say something, but Briggs overrode her.

"This is going to mean big promotions for us," he said, adopting a slightly sniveling tone to his voice.

For just an instant Raya had no idea what was happening, but then she caught on, and she nodded, and mumbled yes.

"I don't care what they say, Comrade Gamov has to be our next first party secretary . . . he just has to!"

Raya nodded again.

"I only hope that I'm on time," Briggs said shaking his head. He led Raya to one of the chairs across the desk from Gamov's, and took the other one.

The door opened, and Gamov strode in. He was dressed in a well-cut, dark suit and conservative tie. He was smiling. The effect made him seem as if he were a good-looking, sleek, streamlined, deadly shark.

"Raya, it's so good to see you again," he said, coming across the room.

Raya and Briggs started to get up, he waved them back, as he went around his desk, and sat down. "Can I get you something? Perhaps a vodka, or a cognac?"

They both shook their heads.

Gamov turned his gaze to Briggs, his slate-gray eyes suddenly the only point of life on his face. "You have not introduced your companion."

"For the past few days I have been Capt. Jan Walcz, special liaison to Gorky Missile Base."

"From Poland?" Gamov asked, his right eyebrow rising.

"Yes, comrade."

"You say . . . for the past few days?"

"That has been my cover, comrade. In reality I am Anatoli Baturin. KGB. Special Investigations Department."

"I see. And who, Comrade Baturin, have you been sent to investigate. And by whom?"

"You, sir. By Comrade Andropov."

It seemed as if Gamov had expected this. A slight smile creased the corners of his mouth. "Yet you have come here. Are you then a traitor?"

Briggs jerked forward so fast he almost fell off the chair. Gamov sat back, his hand going automatically to his right jacket pocket. He had a gun.

"No, sir!" Briggs snapped, as if he was hurt. "No indeed, comrade. I am a patriot who understands that we need a man such as yourself to lead us out of our present contemptible state of weakness. Men like the American president are a menace to world safety, where men like you, Comrade Gamov, are our salvation."

Gamov was beaming, and nodding his head. His hand came away from his pocket, and he sat forward. "You said you had some information for me. Something vital, that concerned . . . Gorky."

Briggs looked over his shoulder at the door. When he turned back, he leaned way forward, and lowered his voice to a bare whisper. "I am afraid to be overheard. This is very dangerous for me . . . for all of us."

"You are safe here, Baturin."

"No one is safe, comrade. Even here there could be microphones." Briggs jumped up and rushed across to a reading lamp on the table, turned it over, and began fumbling with the wire.

"There are no bugs in this room, you fool," Gamov said, jumping up.

"You can never tell, comrade." Briggs snapped frantically. He left the lamp, and went to the door where he fumbled around with the doorframe, and the knob . . . locking it.

"Sit down you idiot!" Gamov roared.

Briggs turned back and rushed over to where Gamov stood, and started to rifle through the items on the desk. Gamov started to push him away; then Briggs brought out his stiletto.

Gamov understood immediately that his life was in danger, and shoved out with all his might, sending Briggs half sprawling over the desk.

Raya jumped up, knocking her chair over. "Jan," she shouted, as Gamov fumbled his automatic out of his coat pocket.

Briggs was on him in the next instant, the thin, razor-sharp blade of the stiletto slipping between the man's ribs, penetrating his heart, killing him instantly.

Gamov stiffened for a moment, then his knees buckled, and Briggs helped him sit in his desk chair, his eyes still open, and only a small amount of blood staining the front of his shirt.

THIRTEEN

Reza Makat sat, sipping a demitasse of very bitter Turkish coffee, as he watched the closed circuit television monitor down the hall from Gamov's study.

He doubted very seriously whether the man who had identified himself as Anatoli Baturin actually worked for the KGB, or for Andropov, but it did not really matter. Gamov was dead. That's all that counted.

What was certain, however, Reza thought as he watched the scene, was that Baturin or Walcz was a professional. He was searching the room, quickly, efficiently, missing nothing of importance except for the television pickups located in the ceiling light fixture (impossible to detect unless the fixture itself was taken completely apart).

As the man went through the desk, item by

item, Colonel Kasin took Gamov's automatic, and pocketed it.

Within minutes, the man had found the safe, and fiddled with the electronic lock for only a second or two before realizing that it would be impossible to open.

"His dirty little secrets are in here," the man said. His Russian was very good. Almost *too* good, as if the man had studied it harder than any Russian studies his own native tongue, which meant he was either a foreigner, or perhaps a dissident poet.

"Let's get out of here," Raya Kasin said. "Every minute we stay decreases our chances of escape."

The man turned back to her. "There is an aircraft waiting for us near the Finnish border."

"What?"

"An airplane. A two-seater. We'll go out low, under their radar. By the time they manage to scramble their jets or rockets, we'll be over the border."

The woman looked fearfully at the door, then back at Gamov's lifeless body slumped in the desk chair. "Let's get out of here. Now!"

The man came away from the safe, stopped in the middle of the room, as if he was thinking of something, as if he had forgotten something, then looked up at the light fixture, his eyes boring directly into Reza's.

He held his gaze there for a long moment, but then shook his head as he turned to the woman.

"What is it?" she asked, looking up.

The man shrugged. "I don't know," he said. "I had the funniest feeling we were being watched."

Reza had to smile. The man was intuitive as well as a professional. He would be fun to play with.

"Let's go," Raya Kasin insisted.

The man nodded. He turned back to the desk, took the phone off the hook, and then they left the study, the man's hand in his right pocket, no doubt on the handle of his very effective knife.

Reza picked up the telephone, and unhurriedly dialed the front gate. It was answered on the first ring.

"Colonel Kasin and her guest have concluded their business. They will be leaving."

"Yes, comrade," the gate guard said.

"They are special guests. Personal friends of Comrade Gamov's."

"I understand, sir," the guard said.

Reza hung up, then left the communications room, and went to the end of the corridor, to the head of the stairs. The man and the woman were just leaving when he looked down. When they were out the front door, Reza turned and went back to Gamov's study, where he flipped on the light, and closed and locked the door. He did not want to be disturbed for the next hour or so.

For several long minutes he stood staring at Gamov's body across the room. He was conscious of the passing time, but he knew there was no hurry. The man and woman were planning on getting first to the Finnish border, and then flying across. That would take time. Many hours, perhaps a day or two.

There was time now. Plenty of it.

Across the room, he opened the safe behind Gamov's desk, carefully avoiding any contact with the body. Inside, he stopped to survey all the films and tapes that Gamov had gathered over the past few years. All of them on celluloid. On plastic. All of them, if not flammable, at least destroyable by fire.

One by one, slowly, methodically, Reza began taking the tapes and films down off the shelves, unwinding them from their spools, and tossing them out into the study, on and around Gamov's body.

Given enough heat, he thought with a smile, the films and tapes wouldn't be the only thing to burn. Afterwards . . . later this morning, perhaps, the terrible murderers of Ilya Gamov, the great Soviet patriot would be found, and brought to justice. And that would be the end of that. Everything would be wrapped up neatly. Gamov would be dead. And justice would be served. No one outside of the Soviet Union could take the credit for the kill.

Raya was holding herself together with great difficulty as they approached the front gate. If there was going to be trouble it would happen here, and Briggs got himself ready for it.

"Easy," he said soothingly to Raya.

The gate guard came out, and pulled the gate open, then stepped back and saluted holding it until they passed.

"I don't believe . . ." Raya started to say, but Briggs held her off.

"Just drive," he said, but he too felt that something was wrong. He was almost a hundred percent certain that Gamov's study was bugged. Probably by himself. Everything that went on in there probably was recorded. The moment after he had struggled and then killed Gamov, he had expected the alarm to be sounded. It hadn't been. The only explanation he could think of was that the recording equipment was automatic. Not manned. If that was so, it could be hours before Gamov's body was discovered, and even longer before anyone there thought to look at the tapes to find out what happened.

Possible, Briggs told himself. Only possible.

They came around the curve and made it out to the highway and back towards Moscow before Raya started to fall apart and Briggs had to drive, pushing the car as fast as he dared.

She smoked and stared out the window as they made it back into the city, but she refused to talk, and it wasn't until they pulled up behind her apartment building that she turned to him.

"We're going up to your apartment. I want you to pack a bag! Have you any money?"

"Some," she said, her voice hoarse. "We won't get away with this."

199

"We're getting out of the country."

"By plane to Finland?" she said, laughing. "Every word we said back there, everything we did, was probably monitored. They'll see that we killed him, and they'll know where to find us."

"Right," Briggs said. "Which is why we're not going to Finland." He got out of the car, then helped her out, and they went up to her apartment.

"What do you mean?" she kept asking him, until they got to her floor and he motioned for her not to say another word.

She nodded after a moment, a little control coming back. But Briggs could see she was still frightened to death. It was one thing going on the run with someone willing and competent. It would be an entirely different story with Raya. God only knew when she'd completely break down.

In silence they went down to her apartment, where she pulled out a small overnight bag and began stuffing things into it—underwear, stockings, slacks, a sweater.

From a bureau drawer she got her internal passport and other travel documents, as well as an envelope containing a small amount of money. These things she stuffed in her coat pocket.

It took less than ten minutes, and when she was ready to go, at the front door, her bag in hand, she turned to look back at her apartment. She put her bag down, and walked slowly back into her bedroom. A moment later she came out with a

200

framed photograph of an older couple, arm in arm, standing on the banks of a river. It was summer. They looked very happy.

She stuffed the photograph into the overnight bag, and they went back down to the car.

It was very late, and no one was up or about, although the Russians have a penchant for staying up until all hours of the morning, talking, eating, singing and drinking.

"And now where do we go in my tiny little car, with license plates that are good only for within a hundred miles of Moscow?"

"To get some help," Briggs said. He took the bag from her, stuffed it in the back seat, and helped her in the passenger side. He got in behind the wheel, and started the car.

"Back to Townsend?" she asked, disdainfully.

"You know him?"

"He was Jerry's control officer . . ." she started. "You're British," she said. "You've been working with them all along." She shook her head. "Was I supposed to fall in love with you, too?"

Briggs pulled away from the parking slot, and headed across town. It was very risky driving at this time of the night. At any moment they could be stopped and their identification checked.

"No, you aren't supposed to fall in love with me. I don't work that way."

"What way, then?" Her fear had turned to bitterness.

"On the basis of trade. You tell me the truth, I do the same for you. You help me out, and I help you."

"I've told you the truth, and I've helped you kill a very powerful man . . . whoever the hell you are. Within hours, maybe sooner, we will be the most wanted man and woman in all of the Soviet Union. So now, what are you going to do for me?"

"Get you out of Russia. It's what you wanted, you told me."

"It's what I want. Only I think it's impossible now."

"Nothing's impossible," Briggs said concentrating on his driving.

"What, are you a magician?"

He smiled. "We'll get out."

It was nearly 3:00 a.m. when Briggs parked the little car behind the ten-story apartment building which contained the apartment for his Jan Walcz cover. The jeep he had driven earlier to get out to Gorky was still there, along with the other vehicles.

On the way over, Raya had told him that she had never actually met Townsend, although Jerry Landers had told her about him.

"Jerry didn't think much of him. Said he was no good."

"Did he talk about anyone else?" Briggs asked.

She shook her head, and was silent for the rest of the trip until Briggs had shut the headlights, put the key under the floor mat and got out. She got out too. "What is this place?" she asked.

"We should be safe here for a little while," Briggs said. He grabbed her bag from the back seat, and they entered the apartment building, taking the elevator up to the third floor.

At the apartment door he listened for several moments, hearing nothing, before unlocking the door and flicking on the light.

He and Raya stepped inside, and Briggs had just locked the door when a sleepy Townsend came out of the bedroom.

"Jesus H. Christ," he said softly, stopping in midstride.

"Splash some water on your face, Bob, you've got a lot of work to do this morning," Briggs said in English.

"Where the hell have you been?"

"No questions now. We need some Russian paperwork. Internal passports. Travel documents. That kind of thing."

"For what?"

"We're getting out."

"You have the MiG . . ." Townsend started, but immediately stopped.

"It's a one-seater. Colonel Kasin and I are leaving together."

Townsend turned to Raya, his eyes lingering on her for several long seconds. "You don't look anything like your photographs."

Briggs nearly leaped across the room at the man, but he held himself in check. For the moment he needed the sonofabitch.

"I want you to get back to Phil. Get the paperwork and return here as quickly as possible."

"It'll take days."

"We don't have days. We'll have to be out of here by noon, sooner if possible."

"What?"

"Gamov is dead."

"How do you know that?"

"I killed him. Out at his dacha. The shit is going to hit the fan at any moment."

"What am I expected to do about it?" Townsend suddenly shouted. "You have your escape route. You can leave the slut here, and I'll . . ."

He never finished the sentence. Briggs was across the living room and on him, his fingers curled around the man's throat, as he shoved him against the wall.

"Go to Phil and do as I say! Immediately, Townsend! Because if you stick around here much longer I shall certainly kill you, without a single shred of remorse!"

Townsend's eyes were wide, his face a mottled red. He nodded, and tried to croak.

Briggs released his grip and stepped back. Townsend started to say something, but Briggs' expression made him hesitate.

"Get out of here, Townsend," Briggs said.

The man ducked back into the bedroom, and when he came out he had his sport coat, and his winter coat. He was angry. "Smythe will get a complete report on this incident. You can't get away . . ."

"If you screw this up, Bob, I'll come after you. Here in Moscow. Back in London. Wherever, whenever, I'll come for you."

Townsend blanched, then hurried out of the apartment.

"What a toad," Raya said in good English.

Briggs smiled tiredly. "More like a bastard."

"Will he do as you ask?"

"I think so," Briggs said. He locked the door, then took off his coat and went into the kitchen. "Are you hungry?" he called out to Raya. "Do you want something to eat. Or drink?"

She had come to the kitchen doorway. "A vodka, or even some wine."

Briggs poured her a vodka and himself some of the Irish whiskey Smythe had provided.

"What did he mean I look different than my photographs?" she asked. "What photographs?"

"I don't know," Briggs lied.

"Yes, you do," she said. "The truth, that's what you want from me, and it's what you promised in return."

Briggs wondered at that moment just how long it would take for Raya's life to straighten around once they got out, *if* they got out. He hoped it would happen quickly.

"They took photographs with hidden cameras. Of you and Jerry Landers."

"When we were . . . together?"

Briggs nodded.

"And you saw these photos? You and that . . . Townsend?"

Again Briggs nodded. Raya was turning red, more from anger than embarrassment.

"The bastards. The dirty bastards." She turned away, her eyes shiny.

"I'm sorry, Raya."

"What did Jerry have to say about it? Where is he, anyway?"

"They sent him back to England yesterday."

"Got him away from the scene of the crime, is that it?" Under stress her English was beginning to falter. "Oh, hell," she said in Russian. She put her drink down, went through the apartment into the small bedroom and laid down on the bed, kicking off her shoes, and burying her head in the pillow.

After a while Briggs came in, and covered her with an extra blanket, then went back into the living room with his glass and the bottle of Irish whiskey. He turned off the light, and sat down by the window, to watch the road below, as the cold wind continued to blow, kicking up the snow.

Reza made sure that the piles of film and tape, as well as Gamov's body, were well soaked with kerosene, before he tossed a match into it, and quickly stepped out into the corridor, locking the door as the room flared up.

He waited there for several long moments, and then leisurely made his way back to the communications room, a grin on his face.

The television image of the inferno inside Gamov's study lasted only a minute or so, before the intense heat destroyed the television camera.

Still staring at the blank screen, he picked up the telephone and dialed for the captain of the guard. The instant the phone was answered, a startling change came over his features. The calm smile was replaced by a look of terror, his mouth screwed up in a grimace.

"It's Gamov . . . Comrade Gamov . . ." he screamed. "They killed him. Oh . . . it's terrible!"

"What is this?" Provnenko shouted. "What's happening?"

"It's Comrade Gamov. In his study. There is a fire. He's dead."

A second later alarms sounded throughout the house.

"It was Colonel Kasin and her friend. They did it. It had to be them!" Reza continued to shout. "I knew it would happen like this. I tried to tell him. Colonel Kasin and her friend. He called himself Baturin, but he also has gone under the name Jan Walcz. He said he was Polish liaison officer of Gorky. You must find them."

There was a great deal of shouting out in the corridor, and the entire house shuddered as the firemen began breaking through the heavy study door.

Reza slowly hung up the telephone, the smile back on his lips as he switched the television monitor to the scene out in the corridor.

He turned the sound down, then picked up the outside phone and dialed for a friend of his at Tass. The world would have to know that Gamov was dead—burned in an accidental fire at his dacha—so that now Yuri Andropov would become the next first secretary.

The sounds of distant sirens woke Briggs from a light sleep, and he jerked up. He had dropped off in the chair by the window. He listened now, as the sirens came closer, his heart starting to accelerate.

It could be nothing, he told himself. Perhaps a fire. Perhaps a crime somewhere.

He got up. He had used the name Jan Walcz in Gamov's study. Someone could have seen the tape by now. They might have figured that Jan Walcz would have an apartment in this area.

The logic was a little thin. Yet he did not dismiss such a possibility as out of the question. The Russians were very efficient at this sort of thing. It was one of the reasons they insisted that all foreigners live in certain buildings in strictly designated areas.

He hurried into the bedroom, and woke Raya, pulling her to her feet out of a sound sleep.

"What is it . . ." she mumbled.

"Get dressed. We have to leave. Now!" Briggs said urgently.

Back in the living room he threw on his coat, and looked out the window as the sirens came closer. Raya came out of the bedroom, one shoe on, the other off.

"What's happening?" she started to say, but then she cut it off, hearing the sirens. Her eyes went wide. "Are they coming here?"

"I think so," Briggs said. "Get dressed!"

As she was pulling on her other shoe and her coat, Briggs grabbed the jeep keys and her overnight bag, and opened the door.

They were coming after Jan Walcz, evidently on the assumption that this was where he would live. They could not know which building, or the apartment number, but they might cut off their means of escape by blocking off all the streets and avenues leading away. If they had the time.

He turned back to hurry Raya when she was at his side. "This may be a bit sticky," he said. "Again, no matter what happens, follow my lead." His gaze dropped to her right hand in her coat pocket. "And whatever the hell you do, don't pull that thing out. You'll get us both killed."

FOURTEEN

The first of the civil police and KGB units were pulling up outside and down the block as Briggs and Raya made it to the front doors on the first floor.

There'd be no way of getting clear of the building, Briggs could see that immediately. As he watched, several units were dispatched to the rear of the half dozen apartment buildings in the foreign section, and still others were arriving.

Another three or four minutes and they might have gotten clear. But not now.

"What can we do?" Raya asked.

Briggs' mind was racing to a dozen different possibilities.

"What is this?" someone demanded from behind them.

Briggs spun around. The old woman he had

met at the elevator the first time he had come here, stood at her open door, her bathrobe clutched tightly at her neck. She was the building manager.

"What is going on? What is all the noise?" she shouted, in Polish.

"It is my wife," Briggs replied in Polish heading across the corridor to the old woman, who shrunk back. "She is sick, and those fools outside have picked this moment to arrest someone."

The old woman looked past Briggs to Raya, who had quickly taken the cue and was holding her stomach. Her eyes were half closed, and she was breathing through her mouth.

"I was just taking her to the hospital," Briggs stammered. "But now . . . I cannot get to my car."

"Come in, come in, you poor dear," the woman said, brushing past Briggs and taking Raya's arm. She led her back into the apartment and Briggs followed, closing the door as the first soldiers came in the front entrance.

"If you have a phone, we can call an ambulance," he said hopefully. The woman's apartment was very large, and well furnished. There was even a small black and white television in one corner.

"Exactly," the woman said, helping Raya to the couch.

Someone banged on the door and the old woman swore. She waddled back across the living room, as Briggs stepped aside, out of the line of sight. He saw that Raya had her hand in her pocket. He reached in his pocket, his fingers curling around the handle of the stiletto.

They banged on the door again. "All right, all right," the old woman screeched in Russian, and opened the door. "What is the noise?"

"Who lives in this apartment, old woman?" a young man snapped harshly.

"I do," the woman said.

"Who else with you?"

"No one else."

"You live alone?" the young man demanded.

"Of course. What do you think?"

There was a great deal of commotion out in the corridor and they could hear someone banging on other doors. The young man went away, and the old woman closed and bolted the door.

"The fools," she muttered. "How are you feeling, my dear?" she asked Raya, who shook her head.

"Please call the ambulance, madam," Briggs begged.

"All right, all right," the old woman said. She moved to her desk in the kitchen and dialed the operator. She asked for an ambulance and gave the address. "How do I know?" she shouted. "A woman is here sick. Am I a doctor?" She listened for a moment, then gave the address again, and hung up. "The fools," she muttered. "They will be here sooner or later."

She went back to Raya's side. "Now, tell me what the trouble is. Where does it hurt?"

Raya said something that Briggs did not quite

212

catch, as he listened to the sounds in the building. They were searching the place. Going door to door. They'd find the apartment soon, and eventually the jeep outside, and Raya's car, and have to conclude that they had come here and were gone already. They'd keep a guard on the building, of course, just in case, and they might even actually search the building again, room by room.

Raya and the old woman seemed to be arguing, softly. Briggs paid no attention. He went to the curtains and carefully looked outside. There where a great number of soldiers, and an even larger number of men in civilian clothes waiting outside.

There was the distinct possibility that when the ambulance showed up, they would not be allowed in, or worse, the soldiers would follow the attendants inside to see who they were picking up.

There was no other way out, though. At least not for the moment.

When he turned around, the old woman was staring at him, a disgusted expression on her face.

"So," she barked. "You are not married to this girl, and yet she is pregnant."

"I . . ." Briggs started, but the old woman wouldn't let him speak.

"It is men like you who have ruined the Russian family. You have no regard for your women or children or love or peace!"

Behind her, Raya looked stunned.

"She is not pregnant," Briggs managed to get in.

"Oh, yes, she is," the old woman insisted. "I am a midwife. I have attended hundreds of birthings. I know. I can tell when a woman is with child." She pointed at Raya without looking back. "And this woman is pregnant!"

Jerry Landers, Briggs thought. The dirty bastard. He never knew, nor had he or Townsend or even Smythe cared to find out. Raya had been nothing more than a piece of baggage, to be used, then stuffed away in some closet.

"I didn't know," Briggs said, looking past the woman at Raya.

"You didn't know . . ." the old woman stopped. She saw the look of tenderness in Briggs' eyes, and misinterpreted it for love. She smiled. "When the ambulance comes, I will get the door," she said, and she went into the kitchen, leaving them alone.

Briggs went to the couch. "How *do* you feel?"

"Fine," she said. "Not pregnant."

"Maybe she's right."

"I hope not," Raya said, but she did not sound too convincing.

Briggs could hear another siren, accompanied by the sound of a bell, in the distance, and he went back to the window.

"The ambulance?" Raya asked.

"I think so."

"But why?"

"You're sick, remember?"

Raya looked toward the kitchen. "You're not

. . . going to hurt her?"

Briggs turned back. "No. I may have to tie her up, but I won't hurt her."

The sound of the ambulance was louder, and the old woman came back. She looked at them both, and then at Briggs.

"Are you two in trouble? Is that why you are hiding from the police?"

Briggs nodded, sheepishly. "We are not supposed to be together. She is the . . . friend of a very powerful man, who swore to put me in jail."

The old woman's eyes widened. "And they are after you two tonight . . . like this? With all this fuss?"

Briggs shrugged. "Maybe not. I don't know."

The ambulance pulled up outside, and Briggs looked out the window. The attendants got out, and pulled a stretcher out of the back, and propped it up on its wheels. They were briefly questioned by one of the civilians, and then waved through.

"They're coming," Briggs said, turning back.

"You're going to send her out. What about yourself?"

"I'm going to tie you up, so they cannot say you helped us. Just let them in, and let me take care of the rest."

The old woman smiled, and nodded. She seemed to be having a good time now that she thought she was part of a conspiracy.

Someone banged on the door, and Briggs stepped aside. The old woman opened the door, and the ambulance attendants came in, pushing the stretcher.

As soon as the door was closed, and locked, Raya sat up with the gun in her hand.

"You will please make no noise, comrades," she said to the flabbergasted attendants dressed in white uniforms. They both put up their hands. The old woman had stepped aside and was grinning.

"Off with those uniforms," Briggs said, stepping away from the wall.

The attendants spun around, then hastily began peeling off their things.

"What now?" Raya asked.

Briggs looked outside. It was dark out, although many of the vehicles had their headlights on. There was some confusion. There were a lot of people scurrying back and forth as the search of the buildings progressed. It would be risky. But they had no other choice.

He turned back, and pulled off his coat. "Get dressed. We're going to be ambulance attendants." He turned to the old woman. "If it hadn't been for you, we would have gotten away," he said harshly. It was for the benefit of the ambulance attendants. He could see that she understood.

When the attendants were undressed, he herded them and the old woman into the bedroom, where he used his stiletto to cut apart a sheet off the bed, and quickly he bound and gagged all three of them.

Back in the living room, Raya was almost

finished dressing. He stuffed a small wad of rubles beneath a couch cushion, for the old woman, then got dressed in the other uniform.

"This is not going to work," Raya said. Her uniform was much too large.

"No other choice," Briggs said. "Just don't do anything or say anything, no matter what happens. We're going to push this cart out of here, down the hall, out the door and into the ambulance. Then we're going to drive away."

"What happens if they stop us?"

"I'll do the talking."

They stuffed their clothes under the stretcher blanket, over Raya's protests. "What if they search us?"

"I'll do the talking," Briggs insisted. "Ready?"

She looked wildly around. "No," she said. "But let's go."

Briggs took up position at the head of the stretcher, Raya at the back, and he opened the door and they went out into the corridor.

There were two soldiers at the front door who opened it for them, and they shoved the cart outside. It was very cold. Men were running back and forth, shouting orders, asking questions. Car engines were running and radios were blaring.

No one stopped them as they pushed the cart back to the ambulance, opened the rear doors and shoved it inside. But a tall, husky man in civilian clothes got out of a car and came over to them before they could close the doors. He was not the same man Briggs had seen talking to the ambulance attendants when they had come in.

"What became of your patient?"

Briggs turned around and smiled and shrugged. "It was the old woman in the first apartment. She does this to us once a month. When we get here her malady suddenly disappears."

The man was looking at Raya who had averted her eyes.

"You should go talk to her, comrade. I think your men have upset her. She would be grateful for the company."

The man looked now at Briggs, who instead of stepping back, moved forward, and lowered his voice, almost conspiratorially, "Tell me, comrade, what is going on here? Are you searching for a fugitive? Should we stay in case someone is hurt?"

"Get out of here," the big man said, suddenly no longer interested in them. He turned and went back to his car.

Briggs slammed the rear doors closed, and he and Raya climbed into the ambulance, started the engine, and headed away.

Raya was shaking. "He was looking right at me," she stammered.

"It's all right now," Briggs said. "We'll be fine, just fine."

They were passed through the roadblocks at the end of the street, and then Briggs, driving as fast as he dared, headed back across town toward the river above Gorky Park, not too far from Solchek's neighborhood, but in a definitely poorer, rougher section.

Briggs kept checking the rearview mirror as he drove, expecting at any minute to see the blue flashing lights of someone chasing after them. But they passed nothing, only two military trucks, and several delivery vans.

As he drove, he also tried to think out their next moves. Heading west toward Finland was definitely out of the question. All roads in that direction would be closed off. The border guards out there would be alerted as well. Escape would be nearly impossible with the increased security.

Conditions to the south wouldn't be much better, either, he supposed, with increased border patrols and rigid checks on all forms of transportation.

There was nothing but the Arctic Circle and the North Pole, to the north, but to the east . . .

"Siberia is bigger than the United States, Donald," someone—one of the Soho emigrés, he thought—had told him long ago. "A million souls are hidden there. Ten million, living their lives unhampered by the fools in Moscow. No one to ask questions, no one to care. It could hold ten times that many."

Siberia and beyond . . . the terminus of the Trans-Siberian Railway . . . Chita, Svodobnyy, Khabarovsk, and then across to Hokkaido. Japan. Freedom.

They would be searching south and west. No one would be looking to the east. The country was too vast. The distances almost unimaginable. No escape that way. No need to close that exit.

The first hints of a gray dawn were coming over the tops of the slum buildings when Briggs spotted what he had been looking for. He pulled the ambulance over to the side of the street, and, before Raya could say a word, jumped out and hurried up the street after a woman he had seen walking by.

She had ducked into a dark alley, and when Briggs reached her, she was vomiting. He waited until she was finished, then helped her to straighten up, and wipe off her mouth.

"You're taking me to the hospital?"

"It's a new government program. You're going to get some better clothes. And a little money," Briggs said, leading the unresisting woman back across the street.

An old man was just stepping out of a doorway, and he looked up at Briggs and the woman as they came across the street. His clothes were nearly as shabby as the woman's. He watched as Briggs brought the woman to the ambulance, then helped her up.

He flipped back the covers on the stretcher as Raya looked in from the front. "Put these clothes on her. Keep her old ones," Briggs said.

He gave the woman a few rubles, as Raya came

from the front to help her, then grabbed his slacks, shirt, and coat from the stretcher, jumped out, and went over to where the old man still stood.

"I have some new clothes for you, comrade," Briggs said.

The old man stepped back fearfully. "I've got no money."

"And I have a few rubles for you. It's a new program from the hospital. Haven't you heard, comrade?"

Within five minutes, just inside the building, Briggs had the old man's clothes, and he hurried back to the ambulance as the woman, now dressed in Raya's clothes, wandered up the street.

He tossed his clothes in the back, then drove south beyond Gorky Park, all the way past Lenin Park, not too far from the Chinese embassy.

Quickly they changed into the disgustingly dirty clothes. Then, making sure no one was around to watch them go, they got out of the ambulance and hurried away from it, ducking down into a subway station three blocks later.

It was fully daylight by the time they got off the subway train on Karl Marx Street well past the Lefortovsky Palace on the far east side of the city. The platform was full with people off to work and children going to school. Although Briggs and Raya were dressed very shabbily, they did not stand out from the crowd. There were many other like them.

Briggs left Raya at a small, overheated café

across from a lumberyard, paid for her tea and rum, and then headed back toward the palace, which at one time held a member of the royal family, but since the revolution housed a museum.

He was very tired. It seemed like years since he had last slept in a bed for any decent length of time, and equally as long since he had eaten a decent meal. He kept to the main street, so that he could blend with the pedestrians. Shops were opening. The schoolyard he passed was brimming with children, all of them in uniform. And there was a good deal of truck traffic.

It took him a half hour to make it over to the Palace Museum, where he circled around the huge stone building to the parking lot in the rear. There were a few trucks, a couple of delivery vans, and a dozen or so small automobiles, mostly Muscovas.

Briggs had figured there would be a number of cars parked here. He came into the parking lot from behind, and screening his actions behind one of the large trucks, he pulled out his stiletto and climbed in one of the cars, quickly picking its lock, and starting it.

Within sixty seconds of the time he had entered the parking lot on foot, he was driving out, and a couple of minutes later he was parked half a block from the restaurant. Because of the way he and Raya were dressed, he did not think it wise to show up at the café in a car. Too many suspicions would have risen.

She was waiting outside for him when he

showed up. Silently they headed back to the car.

No one paid them the slightest attention as they got into the car. Briggs started it, and they headed out of the city to the east. Briggs figured they'd have at least two hours, possibly as many as eight, before the car would be discovered missing. They could cover a lot of distance in that time . . . following the rail lines city by city. When it was time to give up the car, they would travel by train. To the east. To Khabarovsk and whatever awaited them there.

There were a large number of people gathered in the great hall of Gamov's dacha, including the captains of his former guard, the civil police, and several men from KGB . . . men Reza had never seen before.

The morning had broken dull gray, and the wind had continued to rise. Another storm, this one much more intense than the last one, was spreading its way southeast from the Arctic Circle above Finland. Within twenty-four hours very little would be moving in or around Moscow.

All of them in the large room knew this. And they understood that by then they would either have the assassins of Ilya Gamov in custody, or else their heads would roll . . . and the ax would be swung from the highest levels, the very highest levels.

"I am sorry, comrades, but what tape there was of Comrade Gamov's murderers was destroyed in the fire," Reza repeated. "The unit in the communications and surveillance center was not switched on. A simple oversight."

One of the KGB men, Arsenni Orlov, who had been standing by the window, looking out, turned around to face Reza standing by the fireplace.

"You have no idea where they were headed? None whatsoever? Only their names and descriptions?" His voice was harsh, like gravel.

"That is correct, comrade investigator."

"And the films, and tape . . . at least that is what my technicians tell me was all over his body . . . you can tell me nothing about that?"

"Nothing."

"You are lying!" Orlov shouted, taking a step closer.

"And if I am, comrade investigator, what might that tell you?" Reza said calmly. The entire affair was becoming delicious.

Orlov stared into Reza's eyes for a very long time, and when he finally turned away, his right eyebrow was twitching from tension. "Take this man into custody," he said to his people.

Reza stepped back. Provnenko, until recently Gamov's chief captain of the guards, along with half a dozen of his men, jumped up, their hands on their weapons. Orlov's people held up.

"What is the meaning of this?" Orlov screamed.

"I suggest, comrade investigator, that you begin your investigation. I suggest you find Comrade Gamov's murderers very quickly. You are the chief investigator. It would be unfortunate for you if you were unsuccessful in your efforts. Extremely unfortunate. Comrade Gamov was a true patriot of Mother Russia."

Orlov stared at Reza for several more seconds, before he finally turned on his heel, and, with his people, left the dacha.

"When they leave I want the compound secured. I want repairs to the upstairs completed by morning, and I want all officers back here within the hour. We have much work to do."

Provnenko's eyes narrowed. "What work, comrade?"

"Why, catching Comrade Gamov's murderers, of course."

FIFTEEN

It was nearly noon, and the snow was blowing so hard now that it was nearly impossible to see the highway, much less drive, when they came into a tiny village south of Vladimir. They weren't much farther than a hundred miles from Moscow, yet it seemed as if they had been traveling forever. The distance east seemed impossible.

Raya had more or less resigned herself to accept whatever might come her way. From the things she said and from the look in her eyes, Briggs knew that she expected neither to be stopped, nor escape. She simply had no thoughts on the subject. She was merely along for the ride.

It was a form of shock, he knew. In their situation, the most dangerous kind. If a cop turned to her and asked her the time of day, she would tell him everything. It was a syndrome very common to untrained people suddenly thrust into her situation. Its commonness, however, made it no less difficult to deal with now.

Added to that concern was Briggs' worry that the old woman back at the Polish apartment building had been correct, and Raya was actually pregnant. Each time he thought of it he wanted just five minutes alone with Jerry Landers. It was one more glitch in the works.

They stopped at a small farmers' inn, where they had a rough meal of cooked cabbage, dark bread and kvass—a terrible tasting carbonated drink the Russians seemed to love. Then they pressed north the few miles to Vladimir, where they left the car in the vast rally grounds and parking lot of a ball bearing factory.

No one saw them enter the lot by car, nor did anyone notice the ragged couple leaving on foot, trudging nearly two miles through the increasing snow to the railroad depot.

Briggs left Raya on one of the benches as he went around back, outside, to the tracks, where the workman directed him into the depot storeroom where the employees took their breaks. There were four men seated around a large metal stove, sipping their vodka and trying to keep warm. They all looked up when Briggs came in, but only the one in a conductor's uniform bothered to speak.

"Get out of here, comrade. This is for workmen. If you want to get warm go into the depot."

"I would like to speak with you," Briggs said,

respectfully taking off his filthy knit cap.

"I am busy now, go away," the conductor, an older man with white hair said not unkindly.

"This is a matter of very great importance to myself, and to my wife," Briggs said. He looked over his shoulder toward the tracks.

The conductor got up, and led Briggs to another part of the storeroom out of sight and out of hearing of the others. "What kind of trouble are you in, comrade? Where must you run? And how do you intend paying for it?"

"There will be a lot of people looking for us, but we want to go very far east."

"Siberia?" the conductor said, making a joke.

"Yes," Briggs said. "Perhaps beyond."

The conductor's eyes widened. "And rubles?"

Briggs had unwrapped one of the bundles of rubles and he took half of it out of his pocket and started counting. The conductor grabbed the money from Briggs, took more than half of it, giving the rest back.

"Don't flash that much money around, it will be taken from you," the conductor said. "Have you no travel documents then?"

"None," Briggs said.

The conductor seemed to think for a minute. "The Trans-Siberian will come again tomorrow night. It has been ten days since the last, so you are very lucky."

"Where can my wife and I stay?"

"There is a small hotel around the corner. I will send you there. No questions will be asked."

"And tomorrow night?"

"I will be the ticket taker and checker of papers. You will have papers." The conductor's eyes narrowed. "You will have to pay for your tickets separately. To the conductors as far as you want to go. You do understand that?"

Briggs nodded.

"Good," the conductor said. "Now you and your . . . wife go to the hotel, get something to eat, some rest. Your trip east will be very hard . . . very hard the way you will travel."

The hotel was very small and none too clean, but the food was plentiful and tasty, and the landlady agreed to wash and mend their filthy clothes.

Raya was already in bed when the woman came for their clothes and Briggs handed them out the door. When she was gone, he padded over to the chair by the window, a blanket around his shoulders. He sat down, putting his feet up on the edge of the bed.

The chair was uncomfortable, but it was better than the car, and he started to drift off almost immediately, the sound of the wind moaning around the eaves oddly soothing.

"Jan," Raya called his name softly.

He opened his eyes. "What?"

"I'm cold," she said.

He had to smile. "So am I."

"Come to bed," she said.

He sat up and looked across the room at her wide eyes. She was a pretty woman. But she was pregnant.

"It doesn't matter if the old woman back in Moscow was right. It doesn't matter to me," she said.

Briggs got up, and crawled into bed with her. She came into his arms, shivering. "It does to me," Briggs said.

"Then just hold me," she said softly.

The telephone on the main console buzzed softly, and Reza Makat picked it up. "Yes?" he said softly. It was Provnenko.

"We have found the aircraft, comrade. At the extreme northern end of Lake Onega."

Reza had to smile. "They have not arrived as yet?"

"No, comrade. There has been no sign of them. We have the aircraft staked out."

"Very well done, Provnenko. Have you questioned the locals?"

"Yes, comrade. They are stupid peasants. No one has seen a thing." There was a slight hesitation in his voice. "Only . . ."

"Only what?" Reza said.

"There are two of them. A man and a woman."

"That is correct."

"And they said the airplane would be here and it was."

"Yes?"

"But it is a MiG. A jet."

"So what?" Reza snapped, but then he understood what Provnenko was trying to tell him. "It

230

is only a one-seater."

"Yes, comrade. It will only carry one person."

A decoy, Reza wondered? Far too elaborate, he would have thought. "Keep watch on the MiG, let no one near it."

"Yes, comrade. For how long? . . ."

"For as long as I demand!" Reza shouted. He slammed the phone down. He mustn't lose control, he told himself. Not yet. Not now that he was so close. When he handed Gamov's killers on a silver platter to Andropov, there would be rewards. Plenty of them. But until that time his position here was very delicate. He was going to have to watch his step.

He picked up the phone, and dialed for an old friend of his on the Moscow Civil Police Commission. It was nothing more than a hunch, he told himself. But so far their search of Moscow turned up nothing. Five days ago they thought they had them cornered in a building in the Polish section. But they had been too clever. The man had stolen an ambulance, and they had simply disappeared.

Reza and everyone else had assumed simply that the man and woman either were still in Moscow, or were trying to make their way to the plane, or by land across the border into Finland.

How did they get out of the city? And in which direction did they actually head? Those questions had never been fully answered. Yet.

Sitting there, waiting for the connection to be made, however, Reza had the odd feeling that time was running out. Five days. If they had tried for Finland, they'd be long gone by now. But they had not gone that way. They would have been spotted. Which meant they either were still in Moscow, in hiding, or they had gone in another direction. Perhaps by stolen car. Perhaps by train.

They had crossed the Ural Mountains, the vast west Siberian Plain, and now they were back in the mountains that protected Russia's southern borders from Mongolia and, farther east, Manchuria.

To the north were the labor camps that Oumi and his other mentors back in Soho had warned Briggs about. To be sentenced to one of those camps was to be sentenced to a slow, merciless death.

When he had been told that there were no fences around the gulags to keep the prisoners in, he had wondered why there were never any mass escapes. He had often put himself mentally into the picture, knowing that he would simply walk away.

Now, however, actually traveling across the incredibly vast country, he understood why no fences were necessary. Very simply, survival was impossible outside of the gulags. For an unequipped man to attempt to wander across such huge spaces was to invite sure death.

It was on the evening of the seventh day that the train was stopped in the middle of nowhere. Briggs, who had the window seat because it was colder, woke from a light sleep and looked outside. The window was frosted over so all he could see were lights off to the side and forward.

The other passengers in the long car were waking, and looking out, asking what was going on.

Raya stirred in her sleep, and then jerked awake then she realized that something might be wrong. She had been having a hard time of it the past couple of days.

The door at the far end of the car opened and the conductor, a huge, burly man they had picked up back at Krasnoyarsk, came halfway up the aisle, stopping beside where Briggs and Raya were seated.

"There are fugitives aboard this train that the authorities are searching for," the man said in a booming voice.

Briggs peeled off a thick wad of rubles from his dwindling bundle, and surreptitiously slipped them into the conductor's coat pocket.

"You will all please have your papers out and ready for inspection," the conductor said. He glanced down at Briggs. "They will begin their search at the *front* of the train."

The man turned and went back up the aisle and left the car. Briggs could hear men shouting orders outside. Raya gripped his arm.

"They're after us, aren't they," she whispered.

"I think so," Briggs said. "We're going to get off the train, hide outside until they are gone, then get back on."

"They will see us," Raya said. She looked around. "Someone here in this car will tell them that we left."

"No one will say anything," Briggs said. He got up and helped her out of the seat.

No one paid them the slightest attention as they shuffled down the aisle to the rear door of the car. Across the connecting platform, they went through the next car back, which was a Pullman, and then Briggs looked outside.

Forward, near the front of the train, were two helicopters, almost surreal-looking in the artificial light. One of the machines was very large—some sort of troop transport, Briggs figured—while the other was quite small. A personal machine. There were several soldiers standing guard, and people from the first two cars were being herded off the train.

He looked out on the other side of the car, and there was nothing but darkness to the rear, and the glow of the lights on the other side of the train, forward.

They were on some wide plateau. Behind them the tracks disappeared up into the mountains, the thick forest beginning well above them.

Briggs opened the door and jumped down into the snow. It was bitterly cold, the wind strong. He helped Raya down, and together they headed away from the tracks, down a snow-clogged drainage ditch, and up the other side into the relative protection of the deep forest.

About fifty yards in, they stopped, and Raya leaned against the bole of a very large tree. From here, Briggs was able to see what was going on at the train. He hunched up his coat collar and stamped his feet against the cold. It could take hours for the train to be properly searched. They would be able to survive that long out here, but certainly not much longer than that.

Washington, D.C., his desk at the State Department and his tidy apartment across town seemed an impossible distance away at this moment.

"How will we escape, Jan?" Raya asked. Her voice was weak. In the past seven days they had not slept decently, they had not eaten a proper meal, and they had not been able to bathe or in any way clean up. What water was aboard their car was so limited, it was used strictly for drinking.

"When the soldiers leave we'll get back aboard the train."

"I don't mean that," she insisted. "I mean at the other end. At Vladivostok, or wherever we are headed. What then? They obviously suspect we have come this way. They'll be waiting for us." She was beginning to get hysterical.

Briggs came back to her, and took her in his arms. "There will be a way," he said. "They haven't got us yet. In a few days we will be sipping champagne in the sun."

"Yes?" she said, looking hopefully into his eyes.

He nodded. "You can count on it."

The train whistle shattered the silence an hour later, and Briggs stumbled around the tree, his heart leaping up into his throat.

The lights were still there, on the other side of the train. But the train was moving. It was pulling out.

"No," Raya whimpered beside him. "Oh . . . no . . ."

The train was gathering speed as Briggs took a couple of halting steps forward. The train was leaving before the soldiers. It was the one thing he had not counted on.

He could hear the wheels clattering on the tracks now. The whistle blew again, and then the train was past, revealing the two helicopters still parked in a wide spot. The soldiers were piling into the bigger machine and all the lights were going out.

"What are we going to do?" Raya cried.

The big helicopter's engine started with a high-pitched whine that quickly settled into a deep throbbing chop, and slowly the machine lifted into the air, banked toward the north, and then slowly disappeared in the direction the train had gone.

Briggs strained to see through the darkness what was happening with the other machine. But he could see nothing, at first, other than the dull gleam of the plastic bubble, until he caught the flicker of a very small flame, for just a moment.

Someone was down there. In front of the machine. He had just lit a cigarette.

"Come on," Briggs whispered to Raya.

"Where? There's still the other helicopter."

"Quiet," Briggs demanded, taking Raya by the arm. Together they silently made their way closer to the track, just across from the helicopter.

Briggs stopped just within the forest, from here he could see the pilot inside the machine, and another man, very tall, smoking a cigarette outside.

His stance . . . the way he held himself seemed familiar to Briggs.

"Anatoli Baturin—or whatever your real name is—and Colonel Kasin, I know you are out there," the man shouted. Briggs recognized his voice. He was the man who had led them up to Gamov's study.

"The train will not come back. You will surely freeze to death out here before morning. A storm is coming. Give up. You will not be harmed."

What was he saying?

"I watched you kill Comrade Gamov . . . for which Russia thanks you. We have found your decoy MiG near Finland. You cannot escape without my help."

He was right about one thing. They *would* freeze to death out here before morning.

"The soldiers have gone. I have sent them away. They will not come back. It is only myself and my pilot. We will take you to an air force base not too far from here—near a place called Chita. You will be flown out of the country."

"Do exactly as I say," Briggs whispered urgently to Raya. "This may be our chance."

He could feel the old looseness coming over him. It was the same feeling that came over him anytime he was backed into a corner. He was a very dangerous animal at that moment.

Gripping Raya's hand tightly, they stepped out of the woods, across the drainage ditch and up onto the tracks. Reza threw away his cigarette.

"I knew you were there," he said amiably.

The pilot had gotten out of the helicopter and he came over.

Briggs reached back and pulled out his stiletto, hiding it in the folds of his bulky coat, as he and Raya moved closer.

"I'm glad you decided to come out," Reza was saying as he reached inside his coat. "But of course you were foolish to believe me."

Reza had a gun. Briggs shoved Raya aside, and in one smooth motion threw the stiletto, under-handed, the razor-sharp blade burying itself to the hilt in the Russian's chest.

The pilot was digging for his gun, but Briggs was on him, twisting his arm way back, nearly to the breaking point until the man dropped the gun in the snow.

Reza had fallen to his knees and he looked up at Briggs, his eyes nearly glazed over. He tried to raise his gun, but he did not have the strength.

"Who the hell are you?" he started to ask, but

then he pitched forward and lay still.

Briggs shoved the pilot back, and scooped up his gun and Reza's. The man's eyes were wide. He was a helicopter pilot, evidently not a soldier. He was frightened now.

"Nothing will happen to you, comrade, if you cooperate with me completely. Do you understand?"

The man nodded.

"Is there a base at Chita?"

"Yes . . . comrade. A small air force base."

"With MiGs?"

"Yes, with MiGs and others."

Briggs thought a moment. He glanced over at Raya. She would not be able to go much farther. This was it, for them. They either made good their escape now, or they would be done for.

He gave one of the guns to Raya, to hold on the pilot, stripped off his shabby coat, and then knelt down beside Reza's body. He pulled his stiletto out, and cleaned it off, then cleaned as much blood off the coat as he could before he put it on. He pulled on Reza's fur hat as well, then got up.

"Do the people at the base know this man well?"

The pilot looked down at Reza's body. He shook his head. "I do not think so, comrade. I am from the base, I only just heard of Comrade Makat."

"Good," Briggs said. "I'm him, for the moment."

They went back to the helicopter, climbed inside, and within a minute or two they were lifting off, Reza's body a dark spot in the snow.

The pilot banked to the north, and Briggs put the point of the stiletto by his throat. "You will do exactly as I say, or you will die."

The pilot's Adam's apple bobbed. "Yes, comrade," he said.

"How far to the base?"

"Ten minutes."

"Radio in that you are bringing prisoners. That I need a place to interrogate them. Pick a hangar . . . one that contains an operationally ready jet. A two-seater."

"I . . ." the pilot said. But then he reached forward and picked up the microphone.

"Careful," Briggs said, pressing the blade a little closer.

"Chita tower, this is Alpha Bravo seven, incoming," the pilot radioed. He was wearing earphones, so Briggs could not hear the reply.

"Roger. We have prisoners. Comrade . . . Makat is requesting a secured area for a short time."

The pilot glanced at Briggs.

"Roger base. The transport ready hangar. He will require that his aircraft be made ready. Immediately."

Briggs stiffened. What was this?

"Roger base," the pilot said and he replaced the microphone, his lips compressed. He turned to Briggs. "I am coming with you, comrade," he said, "I will fly the plane. The one comrade Makat came in on. It is a small Tupolev troop carrier. We can make Hokkaido easily."

"You are defecting?"

"Yes, sir. If you will have me."

Briggs laughed out loud, and he sat back in his seat. The pilot was telling him the truth. He could see it in the way the man looked at him, by the expression in his eyes. This was no trick. He sheathed his stiletto.

"I can come with you?"

"Why not?"

The Soviet Air Force Base near Chita, about two hundred miles north of the Chinese border, was well lit, and bristled with radar domes, and operational ready hangars. It was a defense base against the day the Chinese attacked them, the helicopter pilot said. There were nuclear weapons and missiles deployed here. It was also one of the bases hooked into Gamov's computer control system.

The pilot brought them low and to the north of the control tower, setting the machine down gently twenty-five yards from an operational hangar, the doors of which were ponderously opening.

"Makat's aircraft?" Briggs asked.

"Yes, comrade."

He looked over his shoulder at Raya. She was on the verge of collapse. "Just a little longer," he said.

As soon as they were down, and the helicopter's motor died, they got out, and Briggs ordered Raya down at gun point.

An officer and a half dozen men leaped out of a truck and hurried over, their weapons drawn.

Briggs turned to them. "Stand back you fools, I have a prisoner," he shouted immediately.

They held up.

The helicopter pilot edged away. If he screwed it up now, Briggs thought, he'd go for the officer first. They'd still have a slight chance.

"We were told there might be two prisoners, sir," the officer said.

"The other one is dead. His body is by the tracks where we left it. You will send a patrol out there immediately to retrieve it," Briggs snapped.

He and Raya came around the helicopter and they stopped a few feet away from the officer and his men. Briggs' right eyebrow rose.

"Well, Captain?" he shouted.

"Comrade?" the officer asked, confused.

"I gave you an order!" Briggs roared. "Get on with it!"

The captain saluted, and he and his men hurried back to their truck. There were other vehicles racing toward them.

Briggs, Raya and their pilot hurried up into the hangar where the ground crew had gotten the small jet transport that Reza had used to come from Moscow ready. They climbed aboard without a word, and the pilot busied himself getting them ready to fly.

The three engines came on one by one, and then they were pulling out of the hangar. A red light was flashing on one of the radio consoles, and the pilot looked around at Briggs who had just come forward after helping Raya strap down.

"They want us to hold up."

"Go," Briggs said, climbing into the right seat and strapping himself in.

The pilot slammed the throttle forward even before they had come all the way onto the runway, and they were accelerating. Briggs switched the radio to the overhead speaker. The tower operator was demanding an explanation. Interceptors would be scrambled.

"Keep going," Briggs shouted, and the pilot hauled back on the yoke as they got up to speed and they lifted off.

Briggs grabbed the microphone. "This is Comrade Reza Makat, I demand to speak with your base commander," he shouted.

The radio was silent for a moment. "Moscow one-three-niner, this is Chita tower, you are requested to make a one-eighty and return to base."

"I demand to speak with your commander. I want to personally thank him," Briggs said.

The pilot kept them low, banked to the east and within a few minutes they had lost radio contact with the base.

"They'll not see us on the radar until the coast.

By then it'll be too late,'' the pilot said.

Briggs replaced the microphone, and smiled. ''I don't think they'll do much of anything as long as they believe I'm Reza Makat. By the time they figure out what's going on we'll be long gone.''

The pilot laughed. "Long gone," he repeated, and there wasn't a hint of regret in his voice.

EPILOGUE

It was morning, and the warm sun shone through the bamboo fence, leaving long stripes across the rock garden and pool. Briggs lay on his back on a futon, smoking. He had watched the dawn, and he was content now to be alone and warm.

His debriefing had been completed two days ago, and Sir Roger had arranged with an old friend for Briggs to stay at this lovely home in the mountains overlooking the sea on the south Japanese island of Kyushu. The only ones here were the house staff, and Briggs wanted to keep it that way.

The pilot who helped them escape was Yuri Sukharev, who had recently returned from duty in Afghanistan. He was already back in the States for his technical debriefing and Rudyard Howard had promised Briggs the man would be well-treated.

Raya Kasin was pregnant, as the old woman back in Moscow had predicted, and she had left five days ago for London. Sir Roger had promised that he and Sylvia would take the girl under their wing.

"The father is Jerry Landers," Briggs had started to explain on the phone, but Sir Roger cut him off angrily.

"I know the whole sordid story, Donald, and believe me, it will be taken care of from this end."

"How about Townsend?"

"We're recalling him from Moscow."

"There's nothing wrong with him except for bad judgment," Briggs interjected. Townsend was an ass, but he wasn't the enemy.

"A rather crippling malady for someone in this business. I think he'll be reassigned to some nice, safe administrative post somewhere."

And that was it. Briggs had not allowed himself to ask about Sir Roger's daughter Sylvia. It was over between them, as it should be. They were from two different worlds—she with a silver spoon in her mouth, and he practically born with a stiletto in his hand.

Lazily, he looked at his watch as he put out his cigarette. It was nearly eight o'clock. Unusual, he thought, for the house staff not to have come sooner.

He sat up, as the rice paper door was slid open, and the bathhouse maid was kneeling there. She was giggling.

"It is time for your bath, O'Meara-San."

Briggs followed the girl across the garden to the

bathhouse, where he pulled off his robe, took a quick warm shower, and then crawled into the very hot, fragrantly-scented water of the cedar tub.

He laid back and closed his eyes, letting the warmth soak into his body, as Rikko, the young bath maid began massaging his shoulders and arms.

It was peaceful, if lonely, here, he thought. And he was in no hurry to return to Washington. There would be plenty of time for that, even though Sir Roger and Howard had both hinted about something that was going to have to be taken care of.

Rikko left for a moment, but when she came back she took up where she left off.

Something intruded in the back of Briggs' mind . . . something gentle . . . something, different.

He opened his eyes. Sylvia Hume was smiling at him. Rikko was gone.

He opened his mouth to say something, but Sylvia, nude, her breasts lovely, moved into his arms.

"Shut up," she said. "You talk too much."

DON'T MISS THE NEXT NEW
MAGIC MAN ADVENTURE!

PIPELINE FROM HELL

Tom Ustinov was a dead man and he knew it. They had been following him for two days now, and last night he had heard the dogs baying behind him. Somewhere across the rock-strewn plain there had been the lights of campfires. He had not permitted himself that luxury. Instead he had ran all night. Heading south toward the Caspian Sea.

The morning had dawned, bleak and gray, a wind rising out of the north. There'd be snow today, Ustinov knew. He had lived in this Godforsaken place long enough now to read the weather pattern.

In fact it had been months since he had come to work for the Trans-Siberian pipeline. Had come to work as a slave to get proof.

He stopped at a jumble of rocks on the edge of a steep hill that fell into an eighty-foot-deep ravine, and laughed out loud. The Caspian Sea was a long ways south, but the company, Langley,

Washington, D.C., and his wife and children were an impossible distance from here.

He had his proof. He had the photographs, and even tapes. A hundred thousand men and women—mostly Jews from Siberia—were working under the most incredibly horrible conditions on the pipeline. Slave labor.

Something intruded on his consciousness. A noise from the north. He turned and shaded his eyes. At first he could see nothing, but then gradually he could make out the helicopter. There were four of them. Fanned out. Coming his way.

Christ, they would be on him any moment. They'd get the photos. They'd know!

Quickly, Ustinov hid the small package that contained the canisters of film, and the tiny tape cassettes in a deep crack between two large boulders. Then he turned and scrambled away from the hiding place, keeping low, heading down the steep hill, mindless of what lay below.

The helicopters were close now, the beat of their rotors filling the morning air. Still Ustinov ran, darting between the large rocks, stumbling, rolling in the sharp rocks, finally picking himself up.

He thought now about his wife and his children. God, he missed them.

Someone else would have to be sent. Someone a lot better than him, because he had tried his best and failed. And those poor people were going to have to be saved.

The lead helicopter, swooping low, passed over him, a spray of gas coming in a long plume out its tail.

Gas! They meant to incapacitate him! They wanted him alive! They'd find the tapes, the film!

As the gas settled, Ustinov redoubled his efforts, making it to the bottom of the steep hill, the deep crevasse suddenly coming up beneath him, and he leaped out into space at the same moment the gas hit him. He lost consciousness as the jagged rocks far below raced up at him. They'd have to send someone to save the poor devils working on the Pipeline From Hell.

THE HOTTEST SERIES IN THE WEST CONTINUES!

MORE FANTASTIC READING!

THE WARLORD   (1189, $3.50)
by Jason Frost
California has been isolated by a series of natural disasters. Now, only one man is fit to lead the people. Raised among Indians and trained by the Marines, Erik Ravensmith is a deadly adversary—and a hero of our times!

ORON #5: THE GHOST ARMY   (1211, $2.75)
When a crazed tyrant and his army comes upon a village to sate their lusts, Oron stands between the warmonger and satisfaction—and only a finely-honed blade stands between Oron and death!

ORON   (994, $1.95)
Oron, the intrepid warrior, joins forces with Amrik, the Bull Man, to conquer and rule the world. Science fantasy at its best!

THE SORCERER'S SHADOW   (1025, $2.50)
In a science fantasy of swords, sorcery and magic, Akram battles an ageless curse. He must slay Attluma's immortal sorceress before he is destroyed by her love.

ORON: THE VALLEY OF OGRUM   (1058, $2.50)
When songs of praise for Oron reach King Ogrum's ears, Ogrum summons a power of sorcery so fearsome that Oron's mighty broadsword may melt into a useless lump of steel!

Available wherever paperbacks are sold, or order direct from the Publisher. Send cover price plus 50¢ per copy for mailing and handling to Zebra Books, 475 Park Avenue South, New York, N.Y. 10016. DO NOT SEND CASH.